Be___ ___ ___ school of teac
Ne_ ___ ___, where he teaches dra___ ___ ___
En___. His novel *Genesis* won the prestig___ ___ Sorcières in
Fra___ce and was shortlisted for the Guardian Children's Book
Prize 2009 and for the UKLA Children's Book Award 2010.
It also won the New Zealand Post Book Award 2007 for Young
Adults and the 2007 Esther Glen Award.

Praise for Bernard Beckett and *Genesis*

'Highly original, this remarkable thriller fuses intricate ideas
with real emotion and suspense. It gripped me like a vice'
Jonathan Stroud, author of the Bartimaeus Trilogy

'Warning – this book may change your life!' *Guardian*

'This novel is witty and compelling . . . unmissable' *Teen Titles*

'Beckett has written a very different young adult novel –
assured, cool, almost cold – it will make smart teenagers
feel very respected' Patrick Ness, author of *The Knife of Never
Letting Go*

'This pure science fiction novel-of-ideas, engaging at every
level, is constru___ ___ ___ ___ ___tly
and successful ___ ___ ___ ___ ___ ___her
thought' James ___

'Bernard Beckett's *Genesis* is a wonderful surprise: at once a fast-paced thriller, a philosophically provocative commentary on the evolution of consciousness and a work of astonishing literary ingenuity' Nicholas Humphrey, *Prospect*

'Beckett raises enough philosophical issues (such as the difference between sentient creatures and computers and when, or if, one segues into the other) to keep an intelligent reader thinking for weeks' Susan Elkin, *Independent on Sunday*

'[*Genesis*] concentrates on the central philosophical argument about the differences between human and machine sentience. Even amidst such dense theoretical territory, Beckett holds the reader with some excellent characterisation, until the closing twists strike with an unforgettable resonance . . . leaving you with a sense that you really have witnessed the advent of something truly original' Jonnie Bryan, *Death Ray* magazine

'By the end you will be completely hooked, desperate to know what happened to Adam and what will happen to Anax. This is one of those books that demands to be read from start to finish' Gareth Jones, SFcrowsnest.com

August

Also by Bernard Beckett

GENESIS

August

Bernard Beckett

Quercus

First published in Great Britain in 2011 by

Quercus
21 Bloomsbury Square
London
WC1A 2NS

Copyright © Bernard Beckett, 2011

First published in 2011 by The Text Publishing Co.
Swann House, 22 William St, Melbourne, Victoria 3000, Australia

Cover design by WH Chong
Illustration by Guy Shield/The Jacky Winter Group

A CIP catalogue reference for this book is available
from the British Library

ISBN 978 0 85738 789 9

1 3 5 7 9 10 8 6 4 2

Printed and bound in Great Britain by Clays Ltd, St Ives plc.

For Clare, with love

PART 1

The Fall

For a moment the balance was uncertain. The headlights stabbed at the thick night. A rock loomed, smooth and impassive, then swung out of the frame. A stunted tree rushed at him, gnarled and prickly. The seat pushed hard, resisting his momentum. Road, rock again, grass, gravel. The forces resolved their differences and he was gliding, a dance of sorts, but he was deaf to its rhythm, just as he was deaf to her screams. Instinct fought the wheel, but the future drew them in.

They were floating, tumbling together in a machine not made for tumbling, weightless and free. He considered the physics: gravity recast as acceleration. An odd thought to have, but what thought isn't odd when death breathes close and sticky? The world slowed. He could not look at her.

The dance broke with a dull thud and the roof above

them crumpled. They bounced. The lights went out and collisions vibrated through him, dissolving the border between feeling and sound. His insides he supposed were acting out their own small version of this greater play. He had heard of it, hearts so determined in their trajectories that they ripped free from their moorings.

With each thud the terrain absorbed momentum. That word again. All is physics. It ended with a shudder. His, hers, the car's. They rocked but did not roll. There in the darkness on a disinterested slab of stone their stories settled into silence.

She was no longer screaming. He was still alive. This was as far as his certainty extended. He considered the possibility he was upside down. Something, perhaps his seatbelt, was digging into his throat. Adrenaline fizzed through him.

The humming untangled itself into distinct sounds. Steam hissed from a punctured pipe. He heard the grating of stressed metal and some part of the engine ticking as it cooled, counting down the seconds. A groan.

Her breath was a warm whisper across his nose. We must be close now, he thought, her head and mine.

He should have said something. It was the polite thing to do. St Augustine's had carved the importance of politeness deep into its charges. *There are no exceptions to this titanium rule. Manners first. Always.*

He was letting the old school down, then; he had thoughts only for himself. A warm stream of blood originating somewhere below his collar trickled up his neck and over his chin (so, definitely upside down). His mouth filled with the taste of salt and iron. A first awareness of pain pulsed through him. Perhaps I am dying, he thought. Certainly he was injured.

He was to blame. She was here because he had brought her here; this point could not be denied. And so, as the rector would have insisted, she was his responsibility. He held his breath to focus on the sound of hers, leaning towards the point where he imagined the mouth might be. Her air came short and fast, shallow with fear. He could detect no bubbling; her lungs weren't filling up. She will live, he decided. The evidence inadequate, the conclusion reassuring.

He reached slowly towards his seatbelt buckle but searing pain beat him back, as sharp and precise as a cleaver.

Something new. A whispering like wind but close, familiar. He stared intently at the blackness, as though the secret of the fragmented sounds was written there. She tried again.

'I can hear you.' Her words landed as spray on his face.

'Sorry.' His inadequate reply.

She was slowly gaining control of her breathing. She swallowed noisily. 'I just meant…you haven't said anything.'

'I was thinking,' he said.

'Thinking what?'

'Wondering. Wondering if I was dying.'

'Are you?'

'I don't know. My shoulder's definitely broken.'

'My head hurts.'

'I think we must be upside down.'

'You don't want to know how it hurts?' she asked.

'I'm not a doctor.'

'Bastard.'

'What do you want, a diagnosis?' The words disturbed his breathing and he ended with a desperate cough.

'I'd settle for an escape,' she said.

'Some say only death can provide that.'

'Some say a lot of shit.'

'How does your head hurt?' he asked.

It wasn't meant to be like this. He'd planned every detail.

'I'm Tristan,' he said.

'You want to know my name?'

'You'll only lie.'

A long silence. Tristan wondered if she had passed out. 'It was the ice. I lost control on the ice,' he said.

Still there was nothing. 'I am sorry.' This time his voice dented. If he could only have that moment back. But which moment? The last moment, before the future sets hard. The hiding place of the soul.

The acrid stench of battery acid touched Tristan's nose. He wondered how this would end, and panic rose in his throat. He spoke only as a way of denying his pain.

'Are you still there?'

'I'm not going anywhere.'

Her voice hovered in the unseen spaces, unnaturally calm. He'd liked it better when she was screaming.

It was wrong to have told her his name. Intimate though their position was, it was no excuse for assuming. This too the rector had explained to the boys. Social ethics was taught at meal time, with their dinner plates steaming before them. They ate only when the rector finished speaking, and he finished speaking only when he was satisfied they had listened. An inspector from the Holy Council visited once during such a lecture but nothing changed. The rector had a way with authority: the powerful lost their nerve around him.

'Are you sure we're upside down?' she asked, out of the cold darkness. Somehow her presence surprised him. How easy, in this tenuous place, to imagine the world in and out of existence.

'I think so. Why?'

'I pissed myself.'

'You shouldn't tell me that.'

She laughed until it threatened her breathing.

'It's not funny,' Tristan insisted.

'We should try to get out,' she said.

'I tried.'

'And?'

'It hurt too much.'

'More than dying?'

'Hard to say.' He imagined her smiling. It strengthened him.

But he did not move. The memory of pain was too fresh, and raw. He heard her wriggling beside him. Something, an elbow, he thought, pressed into his stomach. She grunted with the exertion. There was a hissing sound: air made hard through clenched teeth.

The car lurched and he was thrown into her. She screamed out, a blood-curdling challenge to the silence.

'Sorry.'

His pain had grown indistinct, moving silently through

the body like water searching out its leak. She blew hot air into his face. He could feel her forehead hot and clammy against his cheek. The rector had not prepared him for this.

'So?'

'Door's jammed.'

'Yeah.'

'Yeah.'

Tristan pulled at his mind, seeking the ends of a conversation, but it swelled smooth and indistinct with pain. He waited.

'I smell bad,' she said.

'Doesn't matter.'

'It matters to me,' she said.

'There are better things to worry about.'

'Like?'

'Mortality.'

'We just have to wait until it's light,' she said. 'Then we'll be able to see what we're dealing with.'

'Or someone will see us, from up on the road,' Tristan added, as one adds kindling to a fire, hoping to draw out the blaze. They were close now, to talking.

She rearranged herself so that the full weight of her head was against his cheek. As if they were on a date, wordlessly happy beneath a star-spattered sky. Beyond the piss and shit and blood and burning he found another smell. The smell of her, seeping through her pores, speaking to him. There was a way of making nothing else matter. The easterners had called it meditation, the schoolmen prayer. In the dormitories, where the boys whispered, its name was woman.

She wriggled and her elbow found a broken rib. The pain of it emptied his bladder. Tristan felt the warm trickle running over his stomach. Soon it would reach her.

'Tell me how you got here,' she said.

'The same way you got here. We skidded. The rest is physics.'

'Before that,' she pressed. 'What were you doing out in a car looking for a prostitute?'

It was impolite of her, to mention it. He had been prepared to pretend. For her sake as well as his.

'Come on,' she prompted. 'It's not like you're going to shock me.'

Tristan pressed his lips together, tasting blood again.

'What do you want me to say?' he asked. Ridiculous that a suffering body would find the resources to make him blush, but he felt the familiar heat.

'Tell me what you were thinking. Tell me why tonight. Was it to learn? I think that's it. You've fallen in love with a girl, and you want to appear experienced.'

He was in love. Three years it had been. But she was wrong.

'You wouldn't understand.'

'Explain it then.' Her voice was gentler.

'It's a long story.'

'The night will be longer.'

'I hope you're right.'

There were things he would not tell her, that much he knew. Parts of his story once released into the world would never return, and without them he would be smaller. Five hours earlier that had not mattered to him.

He would not tell her of five hours earlier. The cold sweat as he buckled in, fastening himself to the evening ahead. The drive out into the wastelands, to these very mountains. He would not tell her of the way he followed the illuminated side strip through the settling mist, lost in the trance of switchback on switchback, or of piercing the cloud and seeing, across the eerie white glow of the valley, the great statue rising up above the fog, dominating the City. The Saint: calm, severe, glowing white, *Submission and Salvation* inscribed in the plaque at its feet. He could remember the first time he had read those words for himself.

Tristan would not speak of the way the cold seeped in beneath a stranger's jacket as he stood at the lookout and contemplated his future, or of the way the heathen settlements hummed on the horizon, hot and hopeful.

He wouldn't tell her of the strange calm he felt, standing and stamping to return the circulation to his aching feet. Of how it felt to cruise the streets, the pressing excitement as he practised again the words that would undo him. *What will tonight cost me?* As if he didn't know.

He would not explain to her the way her scent filled the car, or that he could remember to the millimetre the point on her thigh where her dress ended, and how that point rose as she settled against the leather. How his throat went dry, or the way his knee locked as he fought to control the shaking in his leg. And that moment when everything he believed and everything he knew shook and shimmered, the animal within shifting its weight, preparing to pounce. He could not tell her of the fear, the perfect fear. That was his alone.

Tristan felt a sharp stabbing behind his right eye, a pulsing of pain that jumped like static to the back of his skull and exploded in a flash of light. Then it was gone. He strained to take hold of his story, as a drowning man might take hold of a rope. He was determined to drag them both through the night.

'I don't know where to start,' he said.

'At the beginning.'

'I was born.'

'And then what?'

'When I was three, my mother died.'

He felt her head moving against his, as if she was making herself more comfortable for listening, or perhaps to empty her ear of liquid. She would not mention it and he would not ask; already rules were developing.

'Were those events related?' she asked.

'They were to me. They said it was the toxins. We lived in the workers' quarter.'

'I can tell,' she said.

'How?'

'The way you talk.'

'I've spent ten years trying to hide it.'

'It's not long enough. Come on, your story.'

'You have to stop interrupting me.'

'Why?'

'Because it hurts,' he told her, and he was not lying. The words came so puny and sharp he needed all his strength to keep them flowing.

Tristan's Story

By the age of six Tristan knew every dip and twist of the quarter's broken streets. While his father worked at the water treatment plant beyond the swamplands Tristan ran errands for Father Carmichael, delivering the priest's potions to the sick and dying. They paid in coins worn smooth with worry, and Tristan grew up with the smell of death never far from his nose. His father said the workers' quarter had been that way since the war.

Tristan danced down pockmarked streets, proud of the speed with which he could negotiate them. The roads in this part of the City of God weren't worth fixing; there was only the occasional delivery truck to worry about and the procession of floats on the holy days. What little fuel there was, gained in secret negotiations with the outside world, was controlled by the Holy Council, and its drivers had no business to attend to here. It was like living in another century now, Tristan's father said, and the words split his tongue, as if they were coated in acid. He thought he kept his pain hidden from the boy, but Tristan's nature was watchful from the start.

Tristan arrived breathless at the door of Madame Grey's house and banged a rhythm with his fists. Madame Grey was known throughout the quarter; short, wide and regal, she rolled through the streets as if she owned them. She called her home a boarding house but hospice was a better word. There was a bed there for those who could find no other place to die.

Somehow the diseases Madame Grey invited into her home found no quarrel with her. The other boys claimed she was magic, but then Tristan had claimed the same himself for the fun of it, so who knew where the truth lay? From the day of Tristan's first delivery his father had warned him never to set foot inside her house. But the warmth of her hand, the yielding of her great soft bosom when she hugged him, the smell that he imagined other boys found in their mothers—there were days he had turned down her invitation with tears in his eyes.

The door opened. Even with advantage of the small step Madame Grey had no more than a head on Tristan. Her hair was long and greasy, some strands black, others whitening, each falling where it would so that her eyes were veiled and she had to cock her head to look at him.

'Tristan. What do you have for me?'

'A package for Mr Simpson, Ma'am,' Tristan said,

bobbing his head down in careful respect. He did not know why he did this. No one had ever told him to, but each time he faced her he felt it happening.

'Mr Simpson passed in the night, Tristan.'

Tristan looked to his feet and muttered a reflexive prayer.

'But no point it going to waste,' Madame Grey smiled. She thrust out her hand, her one visible eye daring him to argue. Tristan knew what was in the bag: he had seen the priest measuring it out. A dried herb for the pain, shredded like wood shavings, its scent sweet and pungent.

'There will be others, Tristan, who can use it just as well. It will save you coming back here tomorrow.' With her other hand she pressed a carefully folded note into his small palm.

'You are a good boy, that he can trust you in this way. A little extra for a prayer, Tristan, and say one for him yourself. May his soul reach heaven too quick for the devil.'

She touched her forehead in the customary manner and Tristan did the same.

There was movement within and Madame Grey pulled back to the shadows. Two young men, sleeves rolled up, manoeuvred Mr Simpson's gaunt frame through the doorway. Their hands were at his shoulders and his head lolled back, stretching the neck until Tristan was sure it should snap. Tristan backed away, both appalled and fascinated by the way the exposed skin dented to every touch and how the dead man's gums had receded, making his yellowed teeth appear unnaturally long. One of the men noted Tristan's interest and offered a conspiratorial leer.

Tristan turned and ran towards the darkening sky. There

was rain coming. That was good. When it rained Father Carmichael let the boys shelter in the choir loft. When it rained Tristan got to watch the service.

The church was small and spare, well matched to its congregation. Tristan looked down on their ailing heads, the exposed scalps dry and flaking. Only those who could no longer work attended daytime services, and those who could not work did not have long to make their peace with God. There were four other errand boys in the loft. They busied themselves with the usual games, bruising the air with silent farts and shaping obscenities with their fingers. Tristan played along, but his mind was on the lilting sermon. He watched Father Carmichael's bony figure turn, splendid in its priestly robes, and heard his voice grow strong with authority. Father Carmichael was a man who mattered. When he spoke others listened. The exact opposite of Tristan's father.

Tristan loved his father, but he did not wish to become like him. He knew he would not be strong enough to carry the suffering.

Tristan looked at *The Holy Works* open on the altar, its pages extending wider than his young arms could reach. A person who could read a book like that would never need worry about his place in the world. A man with knowledge like that would never go hungry.

After the service, Tristan followed the priest into the sacristy.

'Excuse me, Father.'

The old man turned.

'Tristan, what are you doing back here?'

'I have come to ask a favour.'

'And what favour might that be?'

Tristan paused, understanding at once how important the answer would be.

'I would like you to teach me to read, Father, please.'

Father Carmichael looked away as if he did not trust his first reaction and returned to the task of folding his vestments. Tristan watched the priest's hands. He had not noticed them before. The knuckles were sculpted huge by arthritis, making claws of the fingers. The skin though was smooth like a child's.

'What good do you think such learning would do, Tristan?'

Still the priest did not meet the young boy's eyes.

Tristan considered the question carefully.

'Will you die soon?' he asked.

'I expect so.' A smile took hold of Father Carmichael's face. 'But that does not answer my question.'

'I will not die soon,' Tristan explained. 'I am young. That is why you should teach me to read. That is the good it will do.'

Father Carmichael crouched and ruffled Tristan's hair. He stared, as if he had never seen a boy's face before. Tristan hopped from one foot to the other, bursting with not knowing.

'What will your father say?'

'I don't know. I think he might be pleased.'

Father Carmichael shook his head and Tristan saw sadness in his eyes.

'You must ask him first. I need his permission. Do you understand?'

Tristan nodded.

'And I cannot teach you if you do not practise. Do you promise me you will practise every day?'

'Yes.'

'Are there books in the house for you to practise on?'

Again Tristan nodded, although half of it was a lie. There was only one book: a pocket edition of *The Holy Works*, stuffed in a gap beneath the window to keep out the draught, coated in dust and disinterest.

'Very well. If your father agrees, you can come here early tomorrow morning, as soon as you've had your breakfast. There is little time to waste.'

It wasn't that Tristan did not intend to ask. He rehearsed his question during each mouthful, determined to speak just as soon as he'd swallowed the stringy meat. But the words refused to come free, as if some other great force had hold of them. He felt a tightness in his chest, a crushing sensation. The walls felt closer that night; the acrid smell from the street latrine burned more sharply in his nose. The overhead bulb dimmed and glowed, and shadows pulsed across his father's tired face. The workers' quarter was rationed to one hour's electricity each day. They used it for this—cooking and eating together. When the time was up, they retired to bed.

'How was your day?' his father asked.

'I stayed indoors, as you told me to,' Tristan lied.

This then would be his tactic. He would lie to them both. He was used to it. When he could read properly he would surprise his father with his skill. It would be his gift to him. The plan grew solid as the words slipped free. 'I'm glad I did.

The rain was heavy this afternoon.'

'It was,' his father agreed, carefully dividing the last portion of bread in two and handing his boy the greater share. 'Come on, eat quickly, before the darkness comes.'

Father Carmichael was an enthusiastic teacher. They read together from *The Children's Illustrated History of the Church*. Tristan loved the pictures, rendered in the brightest colours he had ever seen. He read of the early prophets, Plato and Jesus, the crumbling of the Roman Empire and the coming of Augustine. Tristan liked the battle scenes best, the way the artist had captured the blood and pain. He imagined being amongst the soldiers, shoulder to shoulder, holding their line against the crusading Christians. The chapter's final image portrayed a dark-skinned Augustinian hero, bloodied but unwearied, his silver sword plunged deep into the breast of the last of the invaders.

Within five months Tristan was able to read the picture's caption:

> Again God stood with those who stayed loyal to
> Him. And He will stand strong with you too, if
> you are brave enough to accept His call.

Tristan practised his reading whenever he could. Father Carmichael offered to let him take *The Illustrated History* home, but Tristan knew there was no place he could hide it. He struggled his way through the works of the Saint instead. The words Augustine used were not particularly difficult, but the concepts they explored were too dense for Tristan's young brain and he felt it wrinkling with the effort. Will, freedom, destiny, grace and time. He couldn't hope to grasp them. Sometimes he asked Father Carmichael for help with this, and although the priest seemed delighted by his interest, he had the infuriating habit of meeting each question with another of his own:

'How is it, Father, that I can be free, if God knows what it is I will do?'

'Why should it not be like this?'

'Because they do not go together.'

'Why do they not go together?'

'Because they are opposites, Father.'

'Are night and day opposites?'

'Yes, Father.'

'But don't night and day go together?'

'Not at the same time they don't, Father.'

'Ah yes.' And here Father Carmichael would smile and bring the tips of his fingers to his lips in satisfaction. 'And so we come back to time. Always we come back to time.'

Tristan was not dispirited. He knew he was still young, and the prospect of one day understanding excited him. Knowledge sat on his horizon like a mountain waiting to be climbed. As he ran his errands he replayed his conversations with Father Carmichael, sometimes word for word, other times inserting new questions that came to him as he stepped over the cobbles, questions so ingenious that the teacher would be forced to admit defeat.

Tristan found a new feeling taking hold of him,

something lighter than happiness. His thoughts drifted more and more from the present to the future. Hope. That was it, even if he couldn't name it. Hope lifted his gaze and floated his mind. He had no idea what lay ahead of him, but he knew it was something. Something beyond the workers' quarter.

He had only just turned into the street when he heard the shouting. It was his father's voice, raised to a threat, the sound so wrong that it stopped Tristan dead. Wrong because his father did not come home during the day. Wrong because their small room never received visitors. And wrong because when he was angry Tristan's father grew quiet not loud; his mouth closed up and his complaints stuck in his throat. But there was no denying it was his father's voice. Tristan edged forward, frightened and curious. He tried to look through the window but the interior was too dark and he could make out only two figures, adult-sized shadows both turned towards him.

'Tristan! Get in here now.'

The two men faced off, as if contemplating an unlikely fist fight, Tristan's father to the left, Father Carmichael to the right. Tristan slunk to the side wall, one eye on the door. He looked to Father Carmichael, hoping he might explain, but the priest said nothing.

'Is it true, Tristan?' his father demanded. 'Is it true you have been lying to me?'

'About what?'

'So, you've been lying to me about more than one thing, have you?'

'No.' Tristan looked to the ground, digging at the dirt with his bare toe. He was caught in a trap he did not understand.

'Then I'll have none of your questions. Have you been lying to me?'

'Yes,' Tristan admitted, feeling the insistent pressure of a seven-year-old's tears.

'About this?'

His father stepped forward, thrusting the battered copy of *The Holy Works* into his small hands.

'Father Carmichael—'

'Don't blame Father Carmichael.' Tristan had never seen his father like this. Anger inflated him, making him taller, and wider at the shoulders.

'He has been teaching me to read.'

'I know; he has told me. So you can read now, can you? Come on then, read to me. Do it.'

Tristan had imagined this moment many times, but never like this. His hands fumbled with the pages and he felt his future rise up before him, twisting into a shape he did not recognise.

'You are great, Lord, and highly to be praised. High is your—'

His father grabbed the book from Tristan's grasp and hurled it to the ground, spitting where it landed. Tristan's world turned watery.

'Tell him then.' His father prodded at the air that separated him from the priest. 'Tell him what you asked me.'

Through his tears Tristan saw that Father Carmichael remained unnaturally calm.

'I am sorry, Tristan.' The voice was soft and measured.

'I thought you had told him. I asked you to, at the outset.'

'I am sorry,' Tristan stammered. 'I am sorry if I have got you into trouble. I just wanted to read.' He turned to his father. 'I just wanted to read, Dad. I thought you would be happy for me.'

'Tell him!' his father repeated, his eyes fixed on the priest.

'I came here to ask your father's permission. Your work, your reading and your questions, Tristan, they mark you out as an exceptional student. I have been to St Augustine's to make your case. You have been granted a scholarship to study there.'

Scholarships to St Augustine's were rare. They went to the children of the aspiring classes: the nurses, teachers and clerks who could find money for tutoring. But a boy from the workers' quarter? Such a thing was beyond dreams. Tristan waited for the joy that he knew belonged to such an announcement, but none came. He looked to his father, trying to understand the rage he could see still trembling on his lips.

'Do you see, Tristan? He wants to take you from me. When your mother died, they…But I said no. I told them it would never happen, and now…Now they are back again.'

'It is not as you think,' Father Carmichael said.

'Will he be taken from my house for this schooling?'

'Yes, but—'

'Then it is exactly as I think!' his father shouted. 'Tristan, tell him. Tell him you do not want to go.'

Tristan had lied to his father many times, but he could not lie now.

'But I want to go. I would like to go to St Augustine's. It is just that—'

His father would not let him explain.

'Get out then,' he roared, and Tristan knew he would never forget the pain that flashed in his father's eyes. 'Leave with him now and never come back. Go!'

Tristan, his small frame racked with sobbing, did as he was told.

§

She was moving again, her head slipping down to his chest, her shoulder digging into his as she sought an anchor. The pain was too much. He heard the sound of his scream echo itself to exhaustion.

'Sorry,' she said. 'Did I?'

'My shoulder.'

'You all right?'

He wasn't, of course. She knew that. Yet he lied. For politeness. For the rector.

'I'm fine.'

'I was just trying to move my back; it's starting to…'

She didn't attempt to finish the sentence.

'You made me cry,' she said. 'Your story made me cry.'

'I'm sorry.'

'No, I like it.'

'You like crying?'

'Tell me more.'

Pictures of St Augustine's great entrance returned,

magnified once more by the perspective of a small, breath-less boy.

'I started at St Augustine's.'

'And what was it like?' she asked.

'It is all you have heard. And more...'

§

Nothing in Tristan's short life had prepared him for the sights and scents of power. Above his head stone arches strained against the weight of their own existence. Delicate leaves carved from stone twisted their way around thick pillars which served no purpose other than to be twisted about: form for the glory of the Maker. It was grand and it was cold too; he understood this immediately. The floors were hard and the high ceilings curved into darkness. He felt small.

Tristan stood in the middle of the row. Instinct placed him there, humility and caution both tugging in the same direction. The college had sent a list detailing the belongings the boys could bring with them and each of the new entrants stood with the single regulation bag at his feet. Father Carmichael had sourced the items for Tristan and had been careful to pack nothing extra. Tristan saw the other boys had not been so restrained. Their bags bulged against the zips, stuffed with illicit comforts.

The rector was a tall man, with a thick waist, and balding, with a long arrowhead nose and eyes that hovered just on the other side of crossing. Tristan noticed none of these things. He did not notice the way the sash sank beneath the rector's protuberant belly, or the polish of the shoes on his splayed feet. All he knew was that suddenly the rector was standing before the boys, as much a presence as a man. Every one of them took a small involuntary step back. The rector walked slowly up and down the line in which they had waited for thirty-five minutes, the fidgeters like Tristan aching with discomfort.

'Welcome.' His voice was oddly high for such a large man, and his hands, Tristan noticed, were unexpectedly thick and strong. St Augustine's was the City's nursery, the place where its future germinated. The best of these boys would in time become the leaders. They would set the rates, fund the research institutes, write the prayers carved into the stones of the Grand Promenade. The boys held their collective breath as the rector glided by. When he reached the end of the line he waited, the pause perfectly matched to the capacity of small lungs.

'Take your bag,' the rector instructed, 'and place it before the boy to your left. You at the end, take yours to the other end of the row.'

Tristan set his bag at the feet of a boy with a soft fringe and haughty gaze. The recipient's jaw muscles twitched, betraying his attempt to appear unmoved. The boy to Tristan's right was soft and dimpled. He placed his belongings reluctantly at Tristan's feet. Tristan smiled his thanks, but received nothing in return. Whatever the good fortune that awaited him in that bag, there would be a price to pay.

That evening the rector lectured them on the foundations of Augustinian philosophy for three solid hours. At the end he threw questions at his startled audience, probing for weakness. Any boy that could not provide a satisfactory answer was brought to the front and made to pray for God's grace. Tristan was one of only three boys who made no mistakes. Although that was a mistake as well. The hardest people to love are our betters. Many years later the rector explained this to him.

Tristan's attackers waited until the night lights had been extinguished and the brothers had returned to their rooms. A firm hand was placed across his mouth although it wasn't necessary; Tristan knew better than to scream. He was dragged from his bed and taken to the courtyard. There they pushed him up against the fountain. Nobody spoke. The game was simple. They held his head under the water until he struggled. When he struggled they pulled him up and beat the remaining air from his gasping body. On the third ducking he worked it out: stay down, do not resist, find out what it is they want. Tristan pretended to black out, going limp in their arms. They counted to five then hauled him from the water, throwing his flaccid form onto the paving.

The next day one of the older students explained the ritual. Every year the boy who brought the least was subjected to this punishment. Tristan asked why. The boy just shrugged and said, 'It's always been that way.'

§

'And in the beginning, there was envy,' she murmured. She found his hand and gently squeezed it. Broken bones graunched together. He did not complain.

'What about your story?' he asked. His voice was tiring and the memories were swarming, fragmenting and reforming in unreliable patterns.

'My story isn't interesting,' she said.

'It brought you here.'

'A boy and a whore. How's that interesting?'

Tristan tried to rearrange himself; his back had begun to spasm. He was confident he understood where they were now in relation to the cabin. They were lying across the roof, wriggled half out of the possessive grasp of their seatbelts, shoulders and heads as close to horizontal as they could manage, legs forced up by the contour of the seats, which were crushed into a shape something like torture. She was lying across him in a way he couldn't quite picture; the angle of her neck and head, their point of contact, surprised him. In the growing cold—violent shivers erupted without warning—her skin was the only source of warmth.

He wanted to sleep; an ancient, insistent weariness blanketed him. He could not let it happen. That much he knew.

'You have to talk.' She was trying to keep the fear from her voice, but she knew it too.

'I don't know what else to say.'

'Tell me what life was like, inside the college.'

'It is hard to explain. At first it was unreal, and then it became…' He struggled to find the word. He could feel a fog creeping over him. He wanted to get lost in it. He wanted to give in. Again she squeezed his hand, encouraging him.

'And then it became normal. A crushing, wonderful sort of normal. I know that makes no sense. St Augustine's makes many things, but not sense.'

The smell of it came to him: the earthy scent of the prickly gowns they washed by hand each Saturday, the cold pungency of stone untouched by daylight, the fetid thickness of row upon row of boys snoring and farting their way through sleep...

§

Each day the boys were woken early, to pray humbly, eat moderately and work unflinchingly through the sun's angry arc. There were gardens to keep within the enclosure and, once their tenth birthday had passed, chores to complete out in the City. The boys provided services to the grander homes whose owners had once worn the plain brown garments of the college.

When the sun dipped to the horizon attention turned to the lessons. These were divided into three types. The first dominated the boys' time, if not their interest. They were set the task of memorising the first four chapters of *The Holy Works*. At first this seemed impossible. Whole weeks were spent stalled on a single page. The weakest boys were broken by the task and returned in ignominy to their families. The rest were tempted to give up too, but the fear of shame trumped despair.

The second type of lesson consisted of long lectures on history, sometimes delivered by the rector, but usually by a brother with a sharpened face and hands that stabbed at the air as if to fend off the devils he imagined crowding in on every side. There was no shortage of words. It seemed to Tristan that every page he remembered of *The Illustrated History* had been turned into a book of its own. The brother's real passion was reserved for a period not covered by the picture book: the years leading up to and following the war. To Tristan this didn't seem like real history. The war had ended only thirty-five years ago and he had heard his father swapping hand-me-down battle stories with his friends. The brother, though, treated it like any other time gone by, hammering his favourite points with certainty and repetition.

'The troubles didn't start when the fuel became scarce, boys, although many will tell you they did. The troubles started when the fuel was plentiful and we unlearned the lessons of gratitude. Say it with me, boys. Say it with me...'

And so they would intone that evening's aphorism, their young voices binding together with unlikely force: 'God does not turn from us in times of hardship; rather, in times of plenty we turn from Him.'

But the fuel did run low and the weather changed, and then the fighting started. Some turned to God, others to science.

'...and the holy cities had two great strengths, boys: our faith and our determination. The heathens laid siege to our great walled cities and two of them fell, but this, the strongest, could never be taken. They didn't need us; we posed no threat to them or their precious wealth. But they could not stand to know we remained here, our fidelity to the God they had spurned a rebuke they could not ignore. Guilt and jealousy spurred them on, and for five long years God tested the strength of our conviction. Not all stayed the course, boys. By the time He sent the storms that ripped the heathen camps to pieces, only the most faithful remained within these walls. They were the fathers and the mothers of your fathers and mothers. We are built from the very best stock, the loyal and the resolute, and now you come here that through learning you may honour their memory by celebrating all that those in the heathen settlements have turned their backs on...'

Most revelled in the brother's patriotism but Tristan had little taste for empty rhetoric. He secretly looked forward to the lessons the other boys dreaded: the interrogations.

The rector's question-and-answer sessions could last long into the night; on one famous occasion he worried the sun back into the sky. The focus of the inquiry was always the same. Will. The will of God and the will of His creation. Tristan was sure there were only so many ways the paradox could be approached but the rector was indefatigable. The puzzle of time, the mystery of creation, the problem of evil, the enigma of knowledge, the state of the soul, the vexations of probability theory or the nature of God's grace, all reduced to a single question. What does it mean, in a world of God's creation, that man is free to choose between the paths of good and evil? This was not, to the rector's mind, an unanswerable question, but as he never tired of reminding them, neither was it a simple one. The truth he taught them was infinitely subtle and could be approached only through a lifetime of contemplation.

Tristan loved the cut and thrust of the rector's arguments and the giddy moments when the beginning of understanding would writhe and rise within, lured to the surface by a perfectly weighted question. Tristan tried hard not to stand out during these sessions, but it was clear he was one of the top students. Although the other boys did not punish him for his abilities they never forgave him his lowly origins. No amount of schooling could match the sense of social superiority every true collegian learned on his parents' knees.

Tristan became a distant planet orbiting the greater social mass, pulled and pulling, and an uneasy balance was established. He did not complain. Every day he gave thanks for the circumstances that had brought him to St Augustine's. And every night he remembered his father. Although he missed him, Tristan learned to keep his feelings at a proper distance. Restraint, the brothers taught them, was the most noble of the male graces. Once, in a moment of unguarded pride, Tristan boasted that he would never cry again.

But he cried on the day they delivered word of his father's death. The rector broke the news himself, kneeling quietly beside the confused boy, trapping him at his pew as the other boys filed out of the chapel.

'Stay a while longer, Tristan.'

Tristan's heart thumped in fear, although he could not think what it was he was about to be punished for.

'Have I done something wrong?' he asked. He was eleven years old then, a child set on becoming a man.

'There are only two who can answer that question,' the

31

rector replied, 'and I am not one of them. Have you stumbled, Tristan?'

'No, rector, I do not think I have.'

'Well, then you have no reason to blame yourself, Tristan. But remember, all but the first mover has its cause. Now, let us bow our heads and give thanks for your father's life.'

With those words a great crack opened up in Tristan's life. He knelt on the cold stone floor while his entire past was sucked into the void. He was an orphan now with no place left to stand.

Through the roar of confusion he heard the rector's mumbled supplications, and through his shock Tristan realised his own lips were also moving, giving thanks although he felt no gratitude. A lump grew in his throat, as solid and certain as the thought that greeted it. I should remember this moment, he told himself. Nothing in my life will ever matter more than this. He was wrong.

It came to him two years later. The night began like any other, with the rector leading the boys in an interrogation. It was normal for the rector to single out one of the boys for particular attention and this night it was Tristan's turn. Tristan parried the early challenges, hoping the rector might lose interest and seek a softer target, but the rector kept coming.

'Is it enough to intend to change one's ways,' the rector asked, 'or must we wait until the test of the future has been passed before the value of contrition can be judged?'

'The intention to reform, made with an honest heart, is enough,' Tristan replied, missing the trap that had been set, 'or else the priest could not have the power of absolution, having himself no clear view of the future.'

It was a rare mistake and the rector seized on it.

'It is not the priest who offers absolution, Tristan; he is nothing more than the agent of God. And God floats free from the constraints of time and so has little trouble measuring the depth of our resolve. We shall be judged not by our intentions, Tristan, but by our deeds. We reconcile not with our past, but with our future.' The rector's rose voice to grand heights, as if the judgment he was passing was not on the quality of Tristan's argument, but the quality of his soul. 'Tonight, you shall stay behind and complete your recitals.'

Recital was the punishment reserved for the boy who had performed most poorly during the questioning and this was Tristan's first time. The reciter was made to stand at the lectern and give lonely voice to whichever portion of *The Holy Works* the rector chose, while the other boys retired for the night. Sometimes the penance lasted no longer than it took the slowest boy to complete his ablutions. On other occasions Tristan had heard the boy stumbling into his bunk deep in the night, left to weave together what little sleep he could from the scraps before dawn.

Tristan was left for nearly two hours and by the time the rector returned his voice was rubbing dry. The rector stood in the aisle, his face as unreadable as ever, and raised his hand, signalling to Tristan that he might stop. From his high vantage point Tristan noticed for the first time the perfect symmetry of the rector's baldness, the scalp stretched tight and shiny across its bony skull.

'I have been looking at your folders, Tristan. You have a fine hand for illustration.' The rector spoke gently.

'Thank you,' Tristan mumbled, avoiding the rector's eyes. He knew too well how easily the acknowledgment of a compliment could lapse into self-satisfaction. It was not beyond the rector to snare a boy in this way.

'I would like you to draw for me.'

The rector turned without further explanation and it was only when he stopped halfway down the aisle and motioned with his hand that Tristan realised he was to follow.

Tristan was thirteen and considered himself to be the better part of a man. He was proud of his learning, which he believed had trained him to dive deep beneath life's surface. But his education had been as selective as it was demanding. Nothing he had heard or thought had prepared him for what he would find in the rector's study.

'Come in, Tristan.'

The rector beckoned with his oversized fingers. Tristan froze in the doorway, surprised beyond speech or movement.

A girl huddled in the corner as a trapped animal might, her every fibre yearning to become insubstantial amongst the shadows. Tristan could not comprehend it. No female set foot inside the compound. This was the rule, as unflinching as the walls themselves. Even mothers were not permitted to visit. Augustine himself had taught that woman was temptation, the devil's lever.

But she was there, as real as the dark cool stone surrounding her. Tristan stared. For six years he had seen only boys and men. He couldn't not stare. The girl's dark brown eyes darted to the floor, stung by the sin of contact. Tristan remained paralysed, blushing and uncertain.

He waited for the rector to speak again, for order to return, but the rector said nothing, in a way that made it clear that saying nothing was the rule tonight. This was to be an act without commentary, that on completion it might disappear.

The rector pointed to his broad desk of dark mahogany. Laid out upon it was a sheet of the finest sketching paper and a selection of sharpened pencils. Tristan walked unsteadily forward. He breathed in deeply, sat and took a pencil in his shaking hand. He looked down at the paper, willing the girl out of existence, but his disloyal heart knocked a wild reminder of her presence. He could smell her, the scent of an unfamiliar soap.

Tristan felt a drop of sweat form at his hairline and trickle down his temple. The body knew what the mind resisted. From the corner of his vision he could sense the rector sitting in his armchair, knees pointed comfortably outward. An arm swept its instruction and Tristan heard the swoosh of the girl's robe collapsing shapeless on the floor. He dared not look up. In the swirling of his blood he heard the sound of his future arriving.

'Whenever you are ready, Tristan,' the rector purred. 'There's no hurry. Take your time.'

Tristan kept his eyes fixed on the paper he would soon despoil. The shaking of his hands grew wilder.

'That's a shading pencil, Tristan,' the rector said, 'you'll need a finer instrument to capture her form. Look at her, Tristan. Look at her.'

She was not much older than he was, neither girl nor woman, a thing of shadow—a candle-lit ghost whose eyes, fixed on some point behind Tristan's shoulder, were dark and empty. Her body was hungry-thin. He could see her ribs.

'Say if you want her to move, Tristan.'

Tristan's mouth was scratchy dry and he could not speak. In his stomach nerves danced to a tune he had no ear for. A lightness passed through him, a wave of welcome from a part of himself he barely knew.

'Yes, move for us, girl. Your hand, no the other hand, hold that. No, behind you. Now lean into the wall. The leg, the bent leg, bend it more, bring it forward.'

The girl did as she was told, her face painted in shades of fear and concentration. 'Yes, I like that. Start again, Tristan. There's plenty of paper.'

The rector came forward and ripped the first picture, no more than the nervous lines of an early acquaintance, from under Tristan's nose.

'And detail. Don't be afraid of detail.'

Tristan knew what he spoke of. The hair, the nipples: those sights that caused the kicking in his throat.

The face required pure invention. Tristan knew he could not record the things he saw: the animal helplessness, the nature-mocking twist of an empty smile. Terror played at the edges of her eyes, and bewilderment. She did not understand them, these men immune to her sadness. Tristan imagined her lips into a new shape and gave the eyes the warmth of one recognising an old friend.

With every line the dilemma deepened. Tristan knew

what he was doing was wrong but he couldn't summon the will to look away from her. And it wasn't just that he looked; it was the way he looked. At first he had drawn quickly, willing the task to end, but now he lingered, considering the details not as an artist but as a young man, his blood surging with the pounding of an inadequate heart.

The rector did not hurry him. When the picture was complete he stood at Tristan's shoulder, looking from the frightened girl to the paper and back again.

'Well done. Well done. Girl, you may go.'

She gathered up her robe and the rector moved to the stack of books opposite the doorway and pushed it to the side, revealing a hidden passageway. The girl kept her head down, avoiding their eyes, and hurried into the darkness. Tristan ached to follow her, to find some way to apologise and atone.

'You may go to your bed now, Tristan.' The rector nodded once, a small sharp thank you wrapped in a warning.

Tristan's mouth opened but no sound emerged. He lurched from the room.

He couldn't sleep. His mind raced; his thoughts twisted and tangled like the weeds of an unkempt garden. Guilt and lust wrestled one another to exhaustion. Tristan tried in vain to construct noble narratives of rescue and redemption but his virgin imagination foundered on the sharp memory of her body. Every line, every shadow and hollow returned to him, spliced together in a stuttering reel of desire and confusion. He tried to turn his mind to higher things, but it was drawn down by the memory of her. He had never experienced such a powerful sight—one that could take hold of his body, make his heart pound and his skin sweat. His limbs squirmed with the urge to turn themselves inside out. And the blood: the churning, unwelcome blood. He could escape only by returning to her face. Through a mighty act of will he was able to conjure up the terror in her eyes and use her fear to shame his restless body.

§

'Did you come?' she asked him.

'What?'

'When you thought of her, did you come?'

'You're coarse.'

'You hired a prostitute.'

'It's not like you think,' Tristan said. He was surprised that he'd told her this much. He'd lost hold of the telling. Each word pulled the next with it, as if they were linked together in some great chain and their sheer weight dragged the story from him.

'So how is it?'

'I'm trying to tell you but you keep interrupting.'

'Did you hire me by accident?' she teased.

'There are no accidents,' he said.

'What was that?'

'What?'

'Listen, I thought I heard a siren.'

Tristan strained to hear. Her breathing, shallow and slow. His own, thick and fuzzy inside his head. The joints of the chassis creaking, and dripping perhaps, muffled and intermittent. The wind, ripping and dipping through the valley, rushes of fury wrapped in silence. A lamb, bleating, cold and for a moment lonely. But no siren.

'Must have imagined it,' she said. The disappointment settled thickly on them.

'So, back to the girl,' she insisted.

'What girl?'

'The naked girl.'

'I never saw her again,' Tristan said.

'No, but you thought of her.'

That much he couldn't deny.

§

Tristan thought of little else. The next day he worked in the gardens, digging compost into the soil for a new plot of potatoes. The work was hard and repetitive and his head sickened with imaginings of the girl. Her body had faded with the night, but not her frightened eyes. He felt it was a kind of insanity, the way his infected mind brought a stranger so close. Still, he imagined her standing next to him, and in his head explained to her the way the brothers liked their garden. She laughed with him at the institutional fussiness and his ears burned red with gratitude. He heard her approach in the footsteps of other boys, and even composed a poem to her as he worked his spade. But the longer he indulged his weakness the more it made him angry. His head became a battleground and by evening it ached with new wounds.

As the boys filed into the hall for the interrogation Tristan found comfort in the fact that he had been chosen the previous evening. No boy was singled out two nights in a row. It was an unspoken tradition.

The rector prowled before the boys on his small platform. They sat cross-legged on the stone floor, afraid to wriggle or twitch in case they invited his attention.

'So then—' The rector stopped suddenly, as if the idea on his tongue had only just that moment occurred to him. 'This business of the soul. What is the soul, would you say… Samuel?'

Samuel stood, his face edged with cautious relief. He was an older boy, nearing graduation, blessed with good looks and confidence.

The rector began with the easy questions, requiring little more than rote-learnt responses, working up to the greater task in his own good time.

'The soul is that part of the self that exists outside of space and time, in the dimension of God. It is the seat of the will, the centre of responsibility.'

The rector nodded, the signal for Samuel to be seated.

'Yes, and this soul, is it a perfect thing, Christopher?'

'No, for the soul, being of our world, is stained with original sin.' Despite his years at the college, Christopher had never mastered the trick of hiding his nerves. The rector left him standing.

'And so our will is imperfect?'

'Well, yes,' Christopher conceded.

'In what way?'

'It is our will that allows us to divert from the path of God.'

'But is not the choice to move away from God's love the work of an irrational mind?'

The question followed quickly. This was the rector's technique, moving without warning from conversation to bombardment.

'Yes…' Christopher drew the word out as he tried to control a stammer. 'We are capable of acting irrationally. It is one of the choices open to us.'

'And so should not the blame for the choices of an irrational mind lie with He who made the mind irrational?'

The rector was like one of the old paintings that hung in the great hall. No matter where you sat its eyes found you. Even though this was familiar territory the pressure caused Christopher to falter. The rest of the boys silently rehearsed their responses.

'Um, God did not make us imperfect; rather, we chose, at the time of the fall, to embrace imperfection. We were tempted by the devil, and succumbed to his charms. We brought imperfection into the world. God did not turn His back on us; we turned our backs on God.'

It was the answer they had all been taught, yet the rector looked unconvinced. He was the master teacher, determined to unsettle their most comfortable thoughts. Christopher stood in front of Tristan and his shaking was clearly visible. The rector left him suffering a moment longer then nodded for him to sit.

'You have given an answer we all recognise from our

catechisms, and so we cannot call it incorrect. But perhaps we can call it incomplete. Does it not avoid the heart of the problem? Surely you have thought this yourselves. How can we be to blame for turning away from God, when it was God who gave us the capacity to turn? There is a problem here, a difficulty of time, of causation, of blame. Yet you say nothing. Why? Is it because secretly you believe this is a question to which we have no good answer? Such a lack of faith is a terrible thing, boys; you must not yield to such cowardice. We will come back to this. We must come back to this. But not now, for we are not ready.

'Let us move on, then. These things can be approached from many angles. There is another thing about the soul that must interest you. Does every person, Paul, possess a soul?'

Paul stood quickly, sure of his answer.

'No, the people of the night have no souls.'

Tristan felt a wave of nausea break over him. He looked to the ground, certain the rector's eyes were on him.

Everybody in the City knew of the people of the night, but few college boys had ever seen them. Ever since the people of the night had been granted readmission to the City it had been decreed they should enter only during the hours of deepest darkness, when the City's children were cocooned in sleep.

'Why do they have no souls, Paul?' the rector continued.

'In the time of the siege they left the City and tried to join the heathen forces. They turned their back on God, and without God's grace the soul withers like a leaf without sunshine.'

'And why would the heathens not accept the people of the night?'

'God turned the heathen hearts against them. The heathens believed they were spies, sent by us to learn their secrets. Some people thought they carried the plague.'

Like everybody else Tristan knew the story by heart. Families split in two, with half choosing to stay and fight while the others chose to flee and take their chances with the enemy. But those who left found themselves at the mercy of the wastelands and most quickly died. The survivors begged the City fathers to let them return until finally, in a show of great mercy, the Holy Council announced they could visit at night to perform any lowly tasks that might be required of them in return for the right to sift through the City's rubbish. As a final punishment, it was decreed that inside the City walls they were forbidden to speak.

Each night they moved silently past the guarded gate to scrape filth from the paving stones and pull debris from the drains. Tristan remembered lying in bed as a child hearing their shuffling feet and creaking wagon wheels moving past the window, imagining them as great insects, emerging from their decaying underworld to cleanse that which no one else would touch.

But they were not insects. Their thoughts flowed freely through bodies as warm as his own and their eyes flickered with the same uncertainties. She was one of them, the girl he had drawn. The rector had chosen her because she could never speak of it.

'And so what then must we conclude of the will of the

people of the night?' The rector continued and Tristan, barely trusting himself, looked up at his tormentor.

'They have no will,' Paul confidently replied. 'What we see in them is an apparition, just as we might see slyness in a cat, or enthusiasm in a puppy.'

'Yes,' the rector said. 'And yet, if we truly have here creatures without will, then how is it we can continue to hold them responsible for their own failings? Do we not first have to grant them the capacity for failure? Is this not at the very heart of our notion of responsibility?'

It was the type of abstraction Tristan usually revelled in, but tonight he was exhausted and soaked in confusion. He stood up without thinking, feeling somehow detached from his body, as curious as every other boy in the room to see what would happen next. The rector paused. The questions had been rhetorical. He motioned for Tristan to sit.

Breathing ceased and every eye turned to Tristan, captivated by his lunacy.

'It is wrong to say the people of the night have no souls.'

Tristan's trembling voice rippled the air. The rector arched his eyebrows, daring him to continue. And having started, Tristan knew no way of stopping.

'We have nothing but a history of our own invention to support this view. It suits us to believe it. It allows us to mistreat them, but convenience is not truth.'

The words rode on the crest of his rising fury. He had sat close enough to touch her. He had smelt her fear. Now he imagined her watching him, smiling with approval. His eyes watered, his voice and legs shook, but he didn't sit. He waited for the eruption. They all waited for the eruption.

The rector, when he finally spoke, remained inscrutable.

'Work awaits you in the kitchens, Tristan.' Said as if they were discussing a small housekeeping matter. The rector understood the boys would invent implications more terrible than any he could name, just as he understood the value of maintaining the tension. Tristan understood it too. His legs wobbled an uncertain path to the door. For the first time in his college life he felt the warm weight of sympathy.

For six hours Tristan peeled potatoes. He imagined the girl beside him, sharing the burden, sneaking shy admiring glances.

Brother Kevin came in to announce the end of the duty. Tristan guessed Brother Kevin had been specially chosen for the task. He was a kind and humble man, liked by the boys. Tristan burned with shame to be seen this way.

'I have disgraced us all,' Tristan mumbled. 'I am sorry.'

Brother Kevin paused, as if there was something in this simple statement worthy of lengthy consideration.

'Wash your hands and go to bed.'

Tristan walked towards the long stone sink and was surprised to hear the brother following him. Brother Kevin waited until the room filled with the sound of running water, then leaned forward.

'You are not the only one to feel this way,' he whispered.

But that was unthinkable. Tristan kept his head down, concentrating only on his hands and the way they broke the falling water into chaos.

'Did you hear me?' Brother Kevin asked, and Tristan,

too frightened to look up, could only nod. 'I will come for you tomorrow night and you will see.'

Tristan wanted to look up. He wanted to watch the brother leave, to try to read something in the way he walked from the room, but his head stayed down. He watched the water: each drop, no matter the angle of its bounce, still found itself swirling down the drain.

Tristan spent the two hours before dawn in the place between sense and dreams. He thought of her again, and the more he thought, the clearer the memory became. He remembered her in lust and in anger. He imagined brave conversations with the rector, assaulting him with venom and logic. He imagined being called before the Holy Council and, by the power of words alone, reversing its policy on the people of the night. And he imagined her hand, joined with his in gratitude, her skin, smooth against his own. He imagined knowing things that for now were just the beginnings of a rumour, things that made her smile.

Sleep came late the next night, smuggled in on the back of exhaustion. Tristan awoke in darkness to a smooth hand across his mouth. Brother Kevin's. Tristan sat up, his stomach sick with sleeplessness, his mind coated in fur.

'Get dressed and follow me.' The words were whispered so close Tristan could feel their moisture on his skin. He did as he was told, putting on his Augustinian robe and following the brother through the night-quiet halls. They crept to the rector's study and from there through the same passage the girl had used. The tunnel soon became too low for standing and they were reduced to crawling, Tristan with a hand raised above his scalp tracing the rough contours of the roof. Stone and darkness pressed in from every side and he quickly lost all frame of reference. Just when he began to believe he had been lured into a trap they emerged into a world both familiar and strange.

After the tunnel, the muted night lights of the City burned bright and exposing. The streets hummed with the dark industry of the people of the night: kinetic melodies of scurrying, tearing, pulling and sweeping. Their forms were all around, heads down and backs bent to the task of relieving the City of its detritus, paying no attention to Tristan's curious eyes.

'This way.' Brother Kevin motioned for Tristan to follow him. 'Don't worry, they recognise our robes and know better than to touch us. We are perfectly safe.'

They walked past the Grave of the Martyrs, the mound at the eastern end of the City where those who had fallen during the war were buried, then on through the market places, by night stripped of colour and life. Tristan saw a small boy moving on all fours, seeking fallen scraps of food, lapping at the ground with his tongue like a dog. He paused at the shameful sight, but Brother Kevin's hand touched his elbow, urging him on. Then he heard the sound. It came dancing on a breeze—the hint of a choir, children's voices tangled in a single breath—and then it was gone so quickly Tristan thought he might have imagined it. He waited, transfixed, and the sound swooped in a second time.

'They've started,' Brother Kevin whispered. 'Isn't it wonderful? We must hurry.'

The singing came from the Chapel of St Paul. As they drew near they slowed, as if afraid their presence might shatter the melody. Brother Kevin moved into the porch; Tristan followed at his shoulder.

A choir of boys, perhaps twenty in all, gathered before the small altar. They wore the long white tunics of the service boy with high black lace collars which exaggerated their moon-round faces. Their black undergowns were shorter than those worn at service, leaving their legs uncovered from mid-calf to the ground and giving them the appearance of stick people. Their hair was uniformly black and lush, as if they had been manufactured as a batch in some strange musical factory. Tristan guessed they were about ten, too young to understand the impossibility of the sound they created.

It was as if the voices had risen clear of their source. They were no longer the sounds of mouths and throats but had found a life of their own, playing beneath the rafters, mingling for the sheer pleasure of vibration. Voices touching, falling in love, giddy with beauty, and yet entirely, perfectly, unaware.

§

'I am sorry,' Tristan gasped, the memory now jagged with pain. 'It was better than that. It was more beautiful. I, it's just…'

He waited for the word but his mind remained perfectly blank. It was closing in on him, he could feel it. 'This story, there is no point, it is just...'

He felt her shift against him. She was about to speak. He wished she wouldn't, but left her room nonetheless. Manners.

'They were farewelling,' she said, the words falling soft and sure.

'Yes,' he agreed. 'They were farewelling.'

§

Three young mothers stood to the side of the choir, each holding her heartbreak, a small bundle wrapped in the grey swaddling of an unbaptised child. Standing opposite were three women of the night, the stoop of their shoulders suggesting great age. One at a time a mother stepped forward to hand over her dead baby. They received nothing in return, no words, no touch. The crones turned away, leaving the mothers stranded before the altar, mothers no longer. Tristan could barely watch as the hell-bound babies were laid together in a single dark box, their deaths sealed by the voices of angels.

§

Remembering it, Tristan began to weep, as he had on that first night.

'How did it make you feel?' she asked.

'Disgusted, of course.'

'So what did you do?' It was less a question than an accusation. Tristan paused, aware of the absurdity of the answer. But he would give it. The time for not telling had passed.

'I fell in love,' he admitted. 'I had no choice.'

He closed his eyes, embarrassed at how it sounded, how foolish and indulgent. But it was the truth. It was his story. If there was a way of changing it he would have, but they were entangled now, her cheek heavy on his chest, her breath wheezing through him.

'Tell me,' she prompted. Tristan was surprised to hear no judgment in her voice. 'Tell me how it happened.'

Tristan remembered it with perfect fidelity, that moment of distilled need in which he first beheld the church's failure: three mothers beyond consolation, deprived of religion's anaesthetic. What manner of cruelty was it that kept the Holy Council from finding in its shape-changing scriptures a place for these children?

§

The voices of the choir licked at the air, their beauty turned ghoulish.

'Appalling, isn't it?' Brother Kevin whispered. The women of the night moved silently towards a side door with their abandoned freight. The hymn swelled to an unnatural chorus and the mothers were reduced to the roles of extras in their own tragedy. Tristan nodded, not trusting his voice.

'We can't stay much longer,' Brother Kevin said.

But Tristan couldn't move. As if he already knew. As if in

that moment his future had reached out to him and pinned him there.

'All right. You know the way. You must return before the light comes. We will talk soon.' The brother squeezed Tristan's shoulder and was gone.

The choir softened, now no more than wisps of voices twisting through the broken air. Tristan knew he had no place there, a spectator at the frayed edges of grief. The woman in the middle collapsed, racked with sobbing. The death of a child, the most sorrowful of all the mysteries.

Tristan wanted to show himself, to walk forward and offer her comfort. The possibility tugged at him, but he was afraid. The other mothers held their pain tightly to themselves. The leader of the choir raised a hand and the last of the voices stopped, turning the church cold with silence. The choirboys filed out, leaving only the mothers. Tristan was too frightened to move.

He realised he wasn't the only onlooker. A young woman rose slowly from the shadows of a side pew. Tristan pulled back further, watching her move to the altar with quiet grace and purpose. She stopped at the weeping mother. She held out her arms and the woman fell into her.

Tristan strained to make out the young woman's face; she had a shawl wrapped around her head and her features were cloaked in darkness. But he knew. He was sure of it. For three days she had barely left his mind. Brother Kevin had brought him here deliberately. Tristan felt his face grow warm and his stomach turn treacherous.

He was sick with yearning, as if in that first moment of

wanting there was already the seed of loss. He watched her take the first of the women by the arm and usher her to a small door beside the altar. Tristan would follow her now or he would go mad. This, he realised, was how love was, everything made simple and at the same time impossible. He turned and ran out of the church, looping back to the side to intercept her.

The cold air was smudged with mist from the river. Tristan strained to see through the gloom. There was no sign of her.

He banged on the church wall in frustration. He ran his fingers along its wooden surface, seeking out the join of a hidden doorway. There was nothing. His breathing turned shallow and desperate. He pulled at his hair and mumbled his request to the sky.

'Bring her to me,' he pleaded. 'Please God, bring her to me.'

As if in answer Tristan heard footsteps further down the alley, quiet and careful, moving his way. Without thinking he moved to the fence and crouched in its shadows. He watched her approach.

She was alone. Her shawl was pushed back off her face and in the moonlight her pallor was ghostly. Tristan saw his mistake immediately and cursed his foolishness. It wasn't her. The woman from the church, yes, but not the girl from the rector's study.

Tristan stood slowly, coughing so she would see him before she came too close.

The young woman froze. Her dark eyes widened; her

mouth grew small. Tristan raised his hand in apology. They stared at one another, neither speaking, and the moment turned fragile. The face before Tristan and the face in his memory blurred to one. It was ridiculous, he knew. He had the thought, tracked the very words through his head: *this is weak-minded foolishness*. But still it happened. Still this stranger flowed with liquid inevitability into the gap in his heart. He breathed deeply and tried to smile.

Her raised foot, prepared for flight, lowered cautiously to the ground. He saw her shoulders relax. They were two strides from touching. She looked at him quizzically. He gulped at her improbable beauty and looked to the ground, embarrassed and inadequate.

'What are you?' she whispered. He struggled for an answer that might compel her to speak again, but found nothing.

The moment stretched between them and her eyes filled with fear, as if she read in his frozen face some immeasurable danger. She was ready to run. Tristan knew he had to speak or she would leave and take his future with her. His lips moved but no sound came. He saw her eyes narrow as she tried to make sense of him. He knew what would happen next. It played out in a slow-motion torture. She turned from him and fled.

§

'And I didn't follow,' he said, his head swimming now, whether with injury or the memory of loss he could not say.

The night moved closer. He imagined the earth beneath them—beetles scurrying, worms tunnelling through the lines of their lives—waiting.

'My life is heavy with failures, but this is the greatest of them. I did not follow.'

Silence wrapped itself around the admission as if to cushion its collision with the world. Tristan was out of talking. Then the dryness in his mouth brought on a round of retching he could not control. There was no release and he gasped for air, grasping in vain for that space where the pain and fear could not enter. In the darkness he could sense her waiting, preparing to speak.

He had rehearsed the story so often there was no way of knowing which parts belonged to the moment and which had since grown around it like vines taking hold of a tree. But he had never spoken it out loud. Not a word. Nor had he intended to tell it tonight. He waited, his ailing heart knocking out uncertain time.

'You should have followed me,' she said.

'Yes.'

'I was frightened because you did not speak.'

'I know. I should have spoken.'

'My name is Grace.'

'I know that too.'

And so it was finished with, their game of pretending. He waited for more but she held on tightly to her thoughts. *Did you recognise me tonight?* Tristan wished to ask her. *And what did you think of me back then, in the shadows behind St Paul's? Does it sicken you, to know how I thought of you? Can you guess I think it still?*

Would the knowledge have kept you from the car tonight? Does it make you want to laugh or cry that fate has so entwined us? These and a hundred other questions he burned to ask this woman who had taken hold of his dreams, who lay too close too late. But he did not ask them, and she did not speak. Silence was her counsel, and shame was his. Regret roared loud in his ears, great waves of it dismantling him.

Time passed and death did not visit. Tristan heard a gust working its way through the valley below, the pitch rising as it squeezed between mighty walls of rock. The wind ripped over them and a squall caught beneath the exposed chassis, making the whole car shudder. Wherever it was they had landed, it was not the bottom.

'Do you believe in God?' Grace asked him. The question was not strange. They were past strangeness.

'Of course,' he replied. It was easier than the truth, simpler.

She coughed and its sound was the colour of red—heavy drop-laden hacking, clearing the way for another question.

'Why?'

'Because without God,' he started, his voice slipping easily into the lilting rhythm of recitation, 'we have no reason to believe in reason. Without God, our reason is an accident of the cosmos, as ultimately inconsequential as the spinning of the planet or the pulling of the tides. Reason becomes unimportant, and hence untenable. Without God we have only belief, yet we are left with nothing to believe in.'

The line had once delighted him, the way the argument

made a weapon of its opponent's strength.

'And do you believe that,' she asked, 'or is it just the shit they teach you?'

'There is nothing wrong with being educated,' he replied, springing to the defence of the institution that had brought him low. Habit, the ballast that chains a dog to his own vomit. He had read that somewhere.

'Unless you're taught to speak without thinking,' Grace challenged.

'We weren't,' he replied.

'Then you must be a natural.'

'You have a pretty way of talking.'

'You should have stayed on the road,' she replied. 'My talk is nothing.'

'You have a cruel way of talking too,' Tristan said. So this would be the way. They would not mention it. They would pretend it had not been said.

'Pretty cruel. Isn't that what you pay for?'

'I was just beginning to like you.'

'And I hoped it might be love,' Grace joked.

He marvelled at her toughness. 'The two are not exclusive.'

'I'm told liking lasts longer.'

'I have heard that.'

'Perhaps if God had liked us too, this would have worked out better.'

'Where did you learn your blasphemy?' Tristan asked.

'I was born with it.'

'Where was it sharpened?'

'On the streets.'

'Tell me your story.'

'I don't,' Grace replied. 'It's a rule we have.'

'I think we're the exception.'

'All the boys say that.'

'Don't.'

'All right then. You're the first, and I am so nervous I dare not speak. Is that better?'

'You're cruel.'

'You're repeating yourself.'

Her breathing quickened, a series of shallow rapid gasps. Her hand clamped hard to his in terror, reminding him that their talking was a game, nothing more.

Tristan's fear grew more solid, its edges sharper. He felt her moving against him and thought of all the times he had dreamt of such closeness.

'You frightened me,' she finally whispered, letting the words fall with finality, as if this simple admission was all her story needed.

'When?'

'When I first saw you. I thought you were an angel.'

'You don't strike me as the believing type.'

'Things change.'

'I used to believe that,' Tristan said. 'Explain how it happened. Tell me your story.'

'I'm not good at it,' she replied. 'I'm more used to listening.'

'You don't have to do it well,' he said.

'It's clear you don't know me.'

'Such is my failure,' he replied, and imagined her smiling.

'I grew up in a convent,' Grace began. 'Not at first. At first there were four of us: me, my grandmother and my parents. But my mother had lied to the authorities, pretending that she had been baptised. She had been a travelling musician and my father had convinced her to stay. They fled when they were discovered. They would have been executed. It was too dangerous to take me with them. My grandmother lied to the nuns. She convinced them to take me. She was old. She was dying...'

Grace's Story

The strawberry plants were transferred to the gardens on St Augustine's birthday. In the warm years the first crop was ready for the summer solstice. Nobody else had managed to grow strawberries in the City and the nuns made the most of it. The fruit was sent exclusively to the tables of the most powerful, and the secrets of the convent's compost and its prayers were carefully guarded. It was a point of pride with the nuns that no strawberry was ever eaten within the convent walls. The girls spread rumours of the sisters indulging in secret feasts but Grace didn't believe them. The nuns took more delight in depriving themselves than any simple berry could yield.

Good fortune saw Grace selected for gardening duty. She was shy and her reticence was easily mistaken for a desire to be good. Her grandmother had kept a small garden on the common and taught her how to tend it. It was enough. Although the work was callous-hard it was simple and left space in Grace's head for daydreaming. In her third season she was given the honour of preparing the strawberry soil before the compost was added. The success of that year's crop convinced the superstitious nuns that Grace was smiled upon, and the next year she was promoted to the prized role of garden enumerator. Grace was entrusted with completing a stock-take twice a day; the blooming of every flower was meticulously recorded along with the size and state of any fruit. The data she collected was handed to Sister Anne, who was responsible for the ledger in which the secrets of the strawberry were stored.

Grace enjoyed having the nuns' trust, and if it hadn't been for Josephine she might never have been lured to the edge of sin. The nuns discouraged friendship: human closeness was the devil's way of tempting them from their God. Social interactions in the convent were carefully prescribed and monitored. The girls could discuss matters of theology during meeting times and each was permitted to speak quietly to one other girl during evening meals, but only for the ten minutes between service and the sounding of the prayer bell, and always with a nun hovering close.

But the girls found cracks in the system as water finds cracks in a vase. The beds of the dormitory were tightly packed and Grace and Josephine soon discovered that if they reached out in the darkness their hands would meet. It started with them falling asleep with their fingers intertwined. From there a vocabulary developed: taps, squeezes and strokes painted the primary shades of affection and concern. Later Josephine had the idea of spelling out letters on the other's palm, and what began as a game progressed quickly to a shorthand as efficient as any sign language. The two of them would lie awake for hours sharing gossip and dreams and theological speculations no nun would approve of.

Convent life was hard and every girl had her favourite complaint: the endless prayers, the unsmiling nuns, the quashing of talent in the name of modesty and the constant pain from kneeling. But Grace had her garden and her secret friend, and if it had been up to her that would have been enough. Josephine, though, possessed a restless soul.

'It is your birthday soon,' Grace signed on her friend's palm. 'What would you like?'

'I would like to go to a palace to watch the dancing,' Josephine signed back. Dancing was Josephine's obsession. She had been punished more than once for moving with a lightness unbecoming of a devout young girl.

'And if I can't take you to the palace?' Grace asked.

'Then I shall cry all night long and it will be your fault,' Josephine returned. 'And I shall hate you forever, for ruining my birthday.'

They twisted their thumbs together, their signal for a shared smile. Josephine broke off first.

'There is one way you could make it the best birthday ever,' she started.

'How?' Grace asked, delighting at the possibility of pleasing her.

'You could get me a strawberry, from the garden.'

'It is forbidden,' Grace's fingers deftly swept.

'I wasn't thinking we should get caught.'

'They count every bloom.'

'No,' Josephine corrected, 'you count them.'

'They check.'

'Not properly. What would be the point of having you count them if they checked every one?'

'I couldn't,' Grace signed, but already the thrill of transgression was scratching at her.

'Please.'

'I can't promise you.'

'But you'll try?' Josephine's signing grew feverish and hard to decipher. Grace felt the blunt fingernails pressing into her flesh and knew she could not deny them.

A week later Grace spotted the perfect flower. It was the fourth of a cluster and curled back beneath a leaf, hidden to all but the most diligent observer. She would leave it off the register from the outset, figuring that if the nuns were to notice she could claim it was a simple mistake.

They didn't notice. Twice each day she handed over her record sheet and prayed her sins stayed secret as Sister Anne checked each figure against the garden register.

The strawberry remained small, as Grace had hoped it would. It hung low beneath the leaves and was slow to ripen. She would need to pick it early, before it was fully sweet, if it was to remain undetected. She explained this to Josephine, but her friend's excitement was undiminished. They agreed to wait two more days. Sleeping became impossible. They tried to describe what it would taste like but their fingers could not find the words.

When the day came Grace was careful to keep to her routine. She arrived at Sister Anne's station a minute early, as she always did, and stood politely while the elderly nun collected the sheets and joined her in prayers for the garden. The prize grew in the second to last row and Grace knew she must resist the urge to hurry. Her every fibre was drawn tight so that her movements seemed jerky and obvious. She felt eyes on her that didn't exist and the pencil grew thick and clumsy in her hand. She tried to keep track of every other worker in the garden.

It would be a simple manoeuvre; she had practised it often enough in her head. She would crouch before the plant, as she always did, lifting the bunch with her left hand while recording the state of the fruit with her right. While still writing she would hook the fruit with her little finger and pull it free as she stood, pretending to scratch her head and so rolling the strawberry down her arm and inside her tunic. She would store it beneath her armpit. She had practised with a stone, carrying it there without arousing anybody's suspicion.

But Grace had not anticipated how tightly the unripe strawberry would hold its vine. It refused the first tug, and the second. Swallowing the panic, she closed her eyes and pulled again, harder this time, shaking the leaves.

'Grace!'

The voice screamed high across the garden, stopping Grace's blood. Sister Monica bore down on her, her habit swirling behind her like a cape. Grace attempted to hide the fruit but time had fragmented and the world was robbed of smoothness. She held the evidence and the nun, screeching as if to drive out the devil, was only metres away. Grace turned and popped the fruit into her mouth. She chewed once, just enough to register disappointment at the sour unfinished taste, and swallowed.

Sister Monica towered above her, her fury enough to wilt the leaves.

'Yes, Sister?' Grace asked, her voice slipping off the words with trembling.

'The fruit. Where is the fruit?'

'On the plant, Sister.'

'I saw it move. I saw you tugging at the plant.'

'It caught. I dropped my pencil. It became tangled.'

'You're lying to me!'

Sister Monica was a fearsome creature, tall and long-jawed with the flaring nostrils of a horse. Her stare was hard and unwavering.

'Please, Sister, count them,' Grace replied, relieved she had planned this. 'See, in the bunch, three strawberries. Check it with Sister Anne.'

But Grace had underestimated the nuns' great passion for sin. Sister Monica grabbed her by the neck and dragged her not to Sister Anne but straight to Mother Francie's office. Grace grew faint, desperately trying to prepare herself for the questions ahead. But there were no questions. The two nuns consulted briefly before their decision was announced.

'You will be taken to the cell, Grace,' Sister Monica said, her voice thick with satisfaction, 'and you will stay there until all food has passed through you. We will examine your stool for seeds. Or you can confess now. Either way, God already knows.'

'I have nothing to confess,' Grace replied, surprised by the stubborn lie.

'Very well. Follow me.'

Sister Monica carried out the inspections, spreading Grace's shit over a white cloth and examining it minutely. On the fourth day her face rose from its task in triumph. She advanced on Grace, tweezers held before her in accusation.

'A seed, Grace. I have found a seed!'

'But there are many seeds in the garden, Sister,' Grace tried. In four days of thinking it was all she had managed. 'I might have breathed it in, from the compost.'

'Pray for forgiveness, Grace. And for the strength to endure your punishment.'

The whip was made of seven thick strands of black leather, each knotted at one end and plaited into a handle at the other. Grace had seen it used; they all had. Whippings were public affairs.

Grace felt her skin come apart on the first lash and screamed with pain on the second. On the third she fainted. Later, she was told, her limp body was tied to the pole at her wrists and subjected to another five.

She awoke the next day in agony. It took her a moment to realise the screaming voice floating above her was her own. She tried to roll but her back had scabbed to the bed. She felt cracked hands on her brow. Sister Angela was standing over her, muttering prayers through her ageless toothless mouth and wiping Grace's face with a cool wet cloth. Grace looked away in shame.

'Are you ready to make a good confession, Grace?' the sister asked. Grace was surprised by the kindness in her voice.

'Yes, Sister.'

'Then with the grace of God you might start again. Hold my hand, dear. Squeeze it tight. We need to turn you now.'

The wounds ripped open. Grace screamed and felt the old nun's head pressed close against her own.

'Hush, child. Hush. You will get through this.'

'Why are you being so nice to me, Sister?' Grace asked. The kindness confused her. 'After what I have done?'

'God will judge you, not us.' Sister Angela smiled.

'But…but you did judge me. I was whipped.'

'We must oppose the devil, Grace,' the old woman said. 'If we made it easy for you to give in to temptation we would be doing his work for him. Come now, pray with me before the priest comes.'

§

'And I prayed harder than I'd ever—'

Grace was cut short by shuddering, a reverberation so deep Tristan could sense the centre of it, a knot in her tight frightened stomach. He could smell her fear, or perhaps it was his own. He wriggled, painfully finding her shoulder with his hand. He counted the beats of her heart against the ticking of an imagined clock, willing the pace to slow, and praying it would not end this way. Too late now to understand that prayer was not supplication but desperation.

Whatever had brought the shock was passing. He felt her lips against his cheek as he pressed forward to hear her breathing. Even, no longer panicked.

'I'm all right now. It's passed…' Her voice dropped, as if in apology.

'Did you hate them?'

'Who?'

'The nuns who whipped you.'

'No, I didn't hate them. I was young. I believed what they told me.'

'What changed?'

'I saw you.'

'You're laughing at me.'

'I wish I was. It would be easier.'

§

While the St Augustine's boys were being trained in the skills of logic and oratory, the convent girls were being taught that cleverness was the devil's doing. They grew closer to God not through contemplation but through hard work and humility. They didn't question the point because the nuns were careful to emphasise that questions too were the work of the devil. Whatever Satan's vices, sloth was not amongst them.

Sister Angela, though, was good to her word, and Grace was given the chance to make a new start working in the laundry. The convent earned money taking in washing from the stately homes on the hill. The laundry rooms were thick with steam and Grace ended each shift dizzy with exhaustion. She had no energy for signing with Josephine, even if that were still possible. Grace slept alone now, on a small stretcher at the far end of the dormitory, where she could not infect the other girls with her brush with the devil.

Grace could not define the soul—the contortions of theology left her bored—but she knew what it felt like to lose one. Each day without talking to Josephine her insides withered a little more. Grace spent every moment looking forward to the next time she and Josephine might share a secret smile. But the nuns kept special watch on her, and opportunities were few.

As Grace grew hollow with loss, her friend suffered even more. Grace watched Josephine's walk become a shuffle, and her once proud head bow with the weight of sorrow. Each night Grace prayed to be forgiven for the sin of bringing her friend so low. But she kept one secret even from God: the small pleasure she gained from the knowledge that her absence from another's life mattered that much. Selfish pride. Her guilt tightened inside her, but she couldn't admit it, not to God or to herself.

The beginning of the end announced itself with a cough during silent prayers. Grace saw Josephine's narrow shoulders heaving in her attempts to conceal her distress. The next day the coughing was harsher; it played angrily in the throat and reached deep into the lungs. A nun rushed forward and assisted a doubled-over Josephine from the room. It was the last time Grace saw her.

Two days passed without news and Grace's fear turned to desperation. After the evening meal she approached Sister Monica, who had stayed to supervise the cleaning of the plates. The nun looked at her the way you might look down at a dog that has soiled the path before you, calculating whether to make the effort to kick it. Sister Monica waited for the girl to think again and move on but Grace was determined.

'Shouldn't you be joining the others at prayers?'

'Can I see her, Sister?' Grace asked.

'Who?'

'My friend, Sister, Josephine. She was taken sick.'

Sister Monica smiled then, the coldest smile Grace would ever feel.

'The Good Lord took her this morning, Grace. She is fortunate to have been called so soon.'

Grace fell to the ground, screaming and kicking at the air. It took five nuns and a broken nose to calm her.

The exorcism lasted four days and Grace was barely conscious for most of it. Afterwards she remembered flashes, the smell of incense, the sound of chanting, the cold dripping of holy water on her forehead.

When she recovered, Grace knew only one thing: her friend's death was her punishment. She prayed harder than she had ever prayed, begging God for forgiveness, and for mercy on the soul of Josephine. She imagined her dead friend as an angel with wings and a flowing white gown, her sharp nose always wrinkled in delight and her pale hair, weak and welcome as winter sun, forever glowing.

Grace thought she saw Josephine flitting across the darkened halls. At night, as she fell close to sleep, she believed Josephine sat beside her, signing cold messages on her palm. The holy books left Grace unmoved, with all their death and suffering, but she grew to love the angels.

Grace was only ten years old then, a child capable of believing in the simplest plans. She would work hard and pray even harder, and God would come to love her again and forgive her for her wickedness. When she was older she would be invited to join the convent and she would dedicate her life to the saving of Josephine's wretched soul.

Her good intentions lasted two devout years. During that time she came to know the approval the powerful reserve for the submissive. It might have gone on longer if not for the problem of the people of the night.

Each year on Good Friday the people of the night were permitted to knock at the convent door, a concession made in the name of the prophet's sacrifice. They came to hawk trinkets fashioned from the City's waste. The girls were each given a small amount of money and allowed to purchase one item.

Grace looked forward to that night for months. Everybody did. There was no problem ignoring the rags and stench of the visitors; they'd had plenty of contact with the broken through their charity work and understood such hardship to be part of God's mysterious plan. The girls were used to the quick darting eyes of the children and hardly noticed the sores they suffered. They closed their ears to the pleading whispers that reached up to them, creepers intent on strangling their host.

Good Friday came and Grace handed over her small coins in a spirit of generosity and holiness. This was the one day a year the girls were allowed to feel special and they weren't about to ruin it with a show of misplaced sympathy. She bought a small wire butterfly from a woman with a furrowed face and small, suspicious eyes. It was perfectly formed and Grace imagined the long careful hours spent bending it into shape. Like all the girls, Grace had a special box where she kept her trinkets, but this year she wasn't adding to the pile. Instead she took the tiny sculpture and left it outside Sister Angela's door. The nun had kept special watch over her since the whipping, and it felt good to be able to repay her kindness. Grace decided not to leave a note with the gift. It was enough to imagine the old woman's smile.

The following night Grace was on duty at the front gate. It was a promotion from the laundry, engineered, she suspected, by the same old nun. The work was easier. She simply had to sit beside the locked gate in case someone came knocking. Most nights nobody did and she was left with her dreaming. If anybody did knock the procedure was clear. She was to ask them their name and if the voice that came back was female Grace was permitted to look down on her from the small slit above the viewing platform. She would ask her business, take her name and then tell her to return in daylight hours. Male voices were to be ignored, although after three months of working the gate Grace was still to hear one.

The knock came and Grace stirred from her almost-slumber.

'Who is it?'

'I need your help.'

It was a young woman. Grace climbed the ladder to the platform which ran at a height a little above her own head and from there peered down through the slot. Grace could see she was holding something up for inspection. It appeared to be a bundle of rags.

'Please,' the young woman said. Thick strands of hair framed her sunken face and her eyes were deep with pleading. 'My child is very sick. There is no hope for him out on the plains. You must help me.'

'I am sorry,' Grace replied, repeating carefully the words she had been taught, 'you must come back tomorrow, during the hours of daylight.'

'We are not allowed in the City in daylight,' the mother replied.

She was one of them, the people of the night. They had no right to knock here. They knew that. Everybody knew that. Grace didn't know where to look, or how to dismiss the woman. Worse than that, she wasn't sure she wanted to. Normally following instructions made Grace feel holy, but there was something about that face—its desperate darkness—and the dreadful shape of her package.

'Please,' Grace asked, although she didn't know what it was she was asking. For the mother and her baby to vanish perhaps, for neither of them to have ever existed.

'Please,' the mother echoed, but with an intensity Grace couldn't match. 'His name is Ronan. If you do not take him, he will die.'

Give me strength, God, Grace recited silently as she had been taught to do in times of trial. *God, give me strength.*

'I cannot take him,' Grace told the woman. 'I am just a girl.'

'Then get someone who can,' the young mother implored.

'It is not permitted.' Grace felt the words' coldness freeze her throat.

The woman moved back a step, and the light fell on her face. Grace recognised the look in her eyes. She had felt it herself. She understood loss.

'He is a baby, just a baby. He has done nothing wrong. He deserves to live.'

Grace made the mistake of looking at the child. He was only a few weeks in the world and she saw in his wizened features the old man he would never become. The little boy's eyes opened momentarily and in his exhausted half blink Grace glimpsed the vastness of the human tragedy. She was no more able to understand the world's cruelty than he was, and, like him, she would never recover.

'I am not permitted to open the gate.'

The mother did not cry. She did not beg. She knew there was nothing left to be gained. She had one choice remaining; she must have known that all along. The woman blanched with the shock of what would come next, even as she succumbed to its necessity.

'I cannot,' she whispered at Grace. 'I cannot take my child away to die.'

The women knelt and deposited her baby on the step and then, surely terrified her resolve would crumble if she lingered, turned and stumbled into the darkness.

Grace clambered down from her post, her body moving to commands her mind couldn't hear. She had the gate's heavy bolt halfway across when her hand was slapped down.

Grace turned to see Sister Angela, the nun's bottom lip trembling, whether in sadness or fury it was impossible to say. The sister moved to the gate and her face, silhouetted now by the orange glow of the security light, turned to blackness. Grace shielded her eyes with her hand, attempting to block out the dirty halo and read the old woman's expression. But there was only age to see, and a mouth tightening around its words.

'What are you doing?' Sister Angela hissed.

'You don't understand,' Grace said, relieved that of all the nuns God had sent her Sister Angela. 'There is a baby. He is dying.'

Sister Angela swayed for a moment, as if uncertain, and the light behind her flashed a warning. Her ancient hands drew the bolt fully back and she opened the gate just a crack, bending down to look closely at the package.

'He is a child of the night,' she pronounced. 'He cannot be saved.'

Grace's head turned clumsy with shock. She shook it, vaguely aware that soon her mouth would open and the trouble would grow deeper. But not as deep as the baby's trouble. This was her one clear thought: *Do not be cowed; he needs you.*

'Are you going to help him, Sister?'

The old woman placed a bony hand on Grace's shoulder and her voice became gentle.

'Your shift is finished. Hurry back to bed.'

'But you won't let him die?' Grace pressed.

Sister Angela turned from her and the light caught the old woman's glistening eyes.

'Go to bed,' she repeated. 'We cannot always guess at His mysteries. I am sorry.'

Grace wanted to scream, to struggle and to rage. She wanted to force them to drag her spitting from the scene, shouting their murder to the sky. The church was wrong and no amount of praying and scrubbing the steps of the sacred places could cleanse it. But instinct kept her quiet. There was another way. She lowered her head in what she hoped would appear to be submission and walked back to her lonely bed. She counted time: she waited.

Although few knew it, all of the holy buildings were riddled with hidden passages, a legacy of the time of war. Grace had discovered a tunnel when she was first recovering from the exorcism. During those days she had drifted uneasily between wakefulness and sleep, prone to the smallest suggestion. Twice she was sure Josephine visited her, and another time she was certain she saw an angel.

It was a dark figure, possessing a male's posture and dressed in the robes of an Augustinian priest. But Grace understood no priest would ever visit the convent at night and in her feverish, childish mind decided she was seeing a vision. The vision flitted past the open door at the end of the dormitory.

She understood immediately that she was meant to follow it. Angels were not seen unless they intended it. She tracked him to the chapel and from there along a hidden passage that ended beyond the convent's wall. The angel did not wait for her, or even acknowledge that he had seen her, but for two years she had remained certain the purpose of his visit would one day be revealed.

And now it was. He meant for her to be able to reach the baby. God wished her to save him.

Grace lay on her bed and listened to the night, as all the girls had learnt to do. In the patterns of breathing and the breeze-scattered tinklings she found her opportunity. She slipped from her bed and made for the passage, so confident in her calling that she felt no fear. Once outside the convent's walls Grace lowered her head and hurried to the front gate, her young breast swelling with pride that an angel should have considered her worthy of this task.

But, as Grace would later find, there are no angels. There is only birth and death and the screaming in between. The small body, lying where it had been left, was already cold.

Grace took the lifeless bundle in her arms. The baby's eyes were closed, as if in sleep. She was struck by detail: the long curling lashes, the small rounded nostrils, the resigned pout of the lips. Like a doll that a master craftsman had laboured over all his life, but more delicate, more perfect than anything man could conjure. And yet discarded. Empty, pointless, dead. Grace felt her breathing falter as the shock came on. She stumbled into the street, tears flowing down her face, no longer caring who saw her or what they made of it. She walked the streets like a lunatic, circling back on herself, the small tragic bundle held close.

Time went by unnoticed until she became aware of an old crone beside her. The woman did not speak. She took hold of Grace's elbow and guided her gently forward. Grace was too weak with confusion to resist and continued as if in a dream until her head filled with the most beautiful music. It was the sweet voices of a children's choir. Grace moved towards it. Then, in what she was sure was some sort of vision, she realised she was not alone. Three others, all some years older, stood beside her, with grief on their faces and death in their arms.

§

'That was my first passing,' Grace said, her voice now little more than a breath across his face. Her story had brought her to exhaustion. 'I thought it was a dream. I…They must have thought I was the mother; they must have. I returned. One night and then another, to give them the same help I was given. It became my calling. I thought the angel had led me there. It's stupid, I was stupid, but I was young, and the convent, it shrinks your thinking.'

She paused, breathing in slow and long. A small cry of pain escaped. Tristan said nothing; they had an understanding now. He remembered again the broken mothers and Grace's delicate frame gliding forward to hold them. His eyes filled with the tears of her rage.

'If you could have held those women,' Grace said, 'you would have understood.'

'I do understand,' he said, more in hope than certainty.

'Shall I ask the question now?'

'If you must,' Tristan said, preparing himself.

'I've learnt not to ruin the mood.'

He laughed nervously, which she took for permission.

'You said you loved me. When you first saw me—that's how you say you felt. So why did I never see you again?'

The question he must answer, and hope that in doing so his own heart wouldn't break.

'I wanted to see you,' he told her. 'There wasn't a day I didn't think about you.'

And, saying it, something detonated inside him, a feeling broad enough to cover the pain. A feeling of lightness, of falling.

Falling in love. Again.

PART 2

The Temptation

It was a scream not of pain but of fear. The hysterical caving-in of the walls every mind recognises as its fate: bewilderment at the accumulation of the past, the impermanence of the body, the bloody-minded insistence of death. Tristan waited. Wherever it was Grace had travelled to, she had gone there alone. Eventually the screaming choked itself to submission. There was a gulping for breath, accelerating to a kind of whimper.

Tristan's hand found her shoulder.

'What is it?' he whispered, worried his voice might be enough to set off the next avalanche.

'I'm frightened.'

Nothing more than that. Simple and unanswerable.

'It's a good sign. It's the place beyond fear we need to worry about,' Tristan bluffed.

'I didn't think there was anything beyond fear,' Grace bluffed back. He heard it in the steadying inhalation, then the rush of her voice, forcing the sentence out in a single breath.

'Exactly. After the fear, there is nothing.'

'Thank you.'

Her body turned rigid as another wave of pain flowed over her. He said nothing, waited for it to pass, thought how quickly the grotesque becomes unremarkable.

'For what?' he asked.

'Talking.'

Tristan could hear the fight in her voice. They were stubborn, the two of them, stubbornly alive. There was a new pain, something like a stitch only it would not remain confined to his stomach. It stabbed upward, into places he'd never been sure about. His heart was there, in behind his lungs; what else, he couldn't say. Whatever it was, the nerves joined the chorus with sadistic fervour.

'What is it?' Grace asked.

'Nothing,' he lied, feeling light-headed as hopeful chemicals flooded his veins, seeking to defend the breach.

'Give me your hand.'

'Leave it,' Tristan told her. 'When light comes there will be doctors. Until then it is best we try not to move too much.'

'No, look, I think I can get free from this. I think I can cut the belt.'

He marvelled at how hope rallied. Grace took hold at the place where his thumb met his hand and guided it gently through the darkness, over the smooth surface of the dress that on the street had shone so brightly. He felt his broken fingers trailing over her warm body, the involuntary twitching of a muscle ticklish to his touch, or something darker; he did not want to think of it. The geography was unfamiliar to him. He thought he detected the cavity of her navel and the gentle rise beyond. He felt something sharp and metallic. She guided his crushed fingers to the ragged edge where the structure beneath them had ruptured.

'Hold this,' she whispered. 'Keep it from slipping back. If you stop it moving, I can use it as a blade—'

An elbow caught Tristan in the eye. If she noticed she felt no need to apologise. He felt the metal edge moving beneath the force of the rasping belt and he tightened his grip. His body tensed to accommodate hers. She worked quickly as he struggled to hold the makeshift blade in place.

Victory was marked with a small grunt.

'Free!' she whispered. Tristan painted a picture of her gleaming eyes.

'Okay, see if you can move…Ow.'

'Sorry.'

The wriggling intensified and Tristan closed his eyes as each movement found another wound.

'What's…'

'If I can just…'

'Can I help?'

'It's just the…No. No no no!'

Banging, loud and insistent. Bone against metal. In her rage Grace was butting against the metal that had them pinned. Tristan found her head and held it with his broken hand but she bucked away, rocking in frustration.

'Shhh,' he said. 'It's okay. It's okay.'

'It isn't.'

She pulled away from his arm, and when he tried to calm her she brought her free leg violently forward, catching his hip with her knee. Instinctively Tristan moved to her, attempting to smother her anger. Beneath them the cab began to rock.

'Don't. You're going to—'

The car lurched. There was a terrifying moment of suspension before it rocked back. Tristan felt the roof changing shape beneath his head. And then the slipping, as loose rocks shifted and the earth let go. They were moving, sliding headfirst into the dark future. Tristan braced for the final impact. They bounced down the slope in hard jagged collisions. It lasted no more than a few seconds, although, in the stretched-out world of panic, he experienced it in hundreds of slices. They rocked, once, twice, then settled. The wind howled and the car shuddered its reply. Tristan imagined them balanced over a precipice. He had seen the sharp walls of the rock-toothed valley. They were a single slip away from death. He didn't dare move.

'Are you all right?' she asked.

'What were you doing?'

'I was angry.'

'We have to be still now. We have to be careful.'

To be still, to choose slow death over the quick end they perched above. *Let me get out of this, God*, Tristan thought, *and I promise…*but he could think of nothing. A god who would strike such a deal was too hard to believe in. He could feel the pounding of Grace's heart at his shoulder. He loved her. He whispered the words secretly to himself, thrilling in her proximity. She, whose broken body he supported with his own. He loved her. She was right to question his long absence, but he had always loved her.

'Tell me the rest of your story,' Grace said.

'You might not like hearing it.'

'Why not?'

'I didn't like living it.'

'I already know the ending.'

'It isn't finished yet,' he pointed out.

'We'll be all right,' she said.

'You don't know that.'

'Time is passing,' Grace replied. 'And we are not. It's the best we can hope for.'

Tristan's Story

Tristan took Brother Kevin's advice and returned before the first light fingered its way across the sky. He emerged slowly from the tunnel, blinking at the brightness. There was a moment before he fully registered where he was, conscious only that he swayed in a bubble outside time, that his past had ended but his future was yet to begin.

The rector stood waiting, a torch in his hand, satisfaction dancing on his face. Minutes earlier Tristan had stepped lightly through the streets; now nausea compressed his stomach and his stance turned fuzzy.

'Welcome back,' the rector smiled. 'I hope the experience was worth it.'

Tristan looked at his feet, embarrassment turning to fear.

'Did you think,' the rector purred, 'that you would be left to defy the church? Do you really imagine we take such little interest in your progress? Some would be insulted by the assumption, but I remember well the deficiencies of youth. Don't worry, Tristan, you will survive your punishment. Your defiance has presented me with an opportunity and now I mean to use it. Follow me.'

Tristan was a child again, a boy without bearings, the ground beneath his feet no longer solid. The rector turned, but Tristan remained frozen.

'Come, boy, I am giving you a second chance. Don't let me down. There is work to be done. I do you this favour and you have nothing to say?'

'Thank you,' Tristan muttered.

'Well then, let us move.'

Tristan did as he was told; without fuss or conflict the angry rebel was brought meekly back into the fold. Such was the rector's genius.

St Augustine's was divided into two sections. The first formed the public face of the institution, encompassing the church, halls, kitchens, dormitories, studies, courtyards and gardens—those places where the boys and visitors were free to roam. The other was the exclusive preserve of those who had taken their holy vows. At the end of the corridor leading to the grotto, the rector turned, not left but right, into the heart of the forbidden zone. Tristan stopped, sure he was not meant to follow. After only a moment the rector reappeared and beckoned to him. Tristan swallowed deeply and with an uncertain step left the world of the college behind forever.

*

Tristan had never seen a room like it. There were no windows. The ceiling, floor and walls were painted perfect white, causing the intersecting planes to merge. Tristan felt as if he was floating. The rector stood in the centre of the room, his dark form a stain on the pristine space, demanding attention. Tristan tried to look away but he could not.

Next to the rector was a ramp the height of his chest and on it sat a polished black sphere the size of a man's head.

'Welcome, Tristan,' the rector smiled. 'You possess a mind of rare quality. It is raw; there is a long way yet for it to travel. In an ideal world perhaps you would be two years older. But then, if the world was ideal, none of this would be necessary.'

Tristan nodded as if he understood. He felt the desire to please rising up in him. He reminded himself that he hated this man and all he stood for. Tristan imagined the young woman from the church was standing next to him, witnessing his bravery, and the thought of her straightened his tired spine.

The rector took a step to his left, to reveal the only other object in the room. Regarding the wall with its stern eyes was a bust of the Saint. Automatically Tristan dipped his knee in genuflection.

'Ah yes, Saint Augustine.' The rector turned to the bust and bowed in acknowledgment, although Tristan couldn't tell if the gesture was genuine.

'Tell me, Tristan, what do you imagine will happen if I release the ball?'

It was only then that Tristan made the connection. The

ramp was aimed squarely at Saint Augustine.

'Come now,' the rector insisted, 'the question is hardly difficult. Can you not imagine?'

Tristan hesitated, his tired brain furiously looking for the trick. For surely the rector did not mean to...

The rector nudged the ball. It rolled to the beginning of the slope and then, with Galilean predictability, accelerated down the incline towards the helpless icon.

The bust disintegrated in a white cloud of plaster. The ball, its momentum now shared with the shattered pieces, rumbled slowly to the wall.

'It is a sin, is it not,' the rector asked, delight spread across his face, 'to deface an image of the Saint in this way?'

'In any way,' Tristan corrected, barely believing what he had seen.

'Indeed. And so my question is this. How should we punish the ball that perpetrated this crime? What would be the appropriate sentence?'

Tristan did not reply. He had sat through enough interrogations to sense a trap but he couldn't make out its detail. The rector continued, untroubled by his pupil's silence.

'Perhaps you do not hold the ball to blame. Perhaps you do not think the ball should be punished at all.'

'I do not,' Tristan conceded.

'And why not?'

It was like being back in the hall, only here there was no chance the rector would turn his attention to another boy. It was just the two of them, a battle pure. The rector leaned forward, as if scanning Tristan's face for some subtle clue.

'Balls do not make choices,' Tristan said, embarrassed at being reduced to the obvious statement. 'They are not capable of it. To be held responsible for our actions, first we must be granted the capacity for choice.'

'Very good,' the rector said. 'And how, if we may continue down this predictable trajectory, can we be sure the ball, when released at the top of the ramp, does not choose to roll down it? How do we know it does not hesitate for just a moment and consider the other possibilities? To not roll at all perhaps, or to veer left at the last moment, or right, or to veer early, or simply screech to a halt before the point of impact? It would seem, at first glance, that any number of choices are open to it. You look doubtful, Tristan. Tell me why.'

'You know why,' Tristan replied, feebly attempting to return fire.

'Ah, but there you are wrong.'

The rector turned from him and paced the room in what appeared to be mad delight, steepled fingers touching the tip of his nose. He halted amid the saintly debris and swivelled, grinding plaster underfoot. 'All my adult life I have struggled with the problem of the ball, Tristan. You assume I have done this for show, a clumsy metaphor upon which to hang my homily, but the truth is I am as perplexed now as I ever was. The ball has so many paths open to it. It takes one and only one. It chooses. And yet we do not call it a choice. We do not hold it responsible. Am I missing something?'

Tristan hesitated. What he was missing would be plain to even the youngest child, but surely that couldn't be right.

'Yes, I think you are.' Tristan's voice was small with caution.

'And what would that be?'

'You are missing that the ball is subject to the laws of physics,' Tristan said. 'When you release it, the forces are unbalanced and so it rolls forward. It is gravity, nothing more. It rolls because it must roll. It has no choice.'

'And we are not subject to these same laws?' the rector asked.

'Of course.'

'And yet we make choices.'

'We do.'

'How do you know?'

A worthy question perhaps, for one who'd never encountered it. But Tristan was a St Augustine's student and his education had consisted of little but this question. The familiarity relaxed him and he felt a sharpening of his thoughts.

'When I decide something I am aware of the options. Options that no physics precludes. Sometimes, when faced with a choice, I move left. Other times, I move right. Physics allows either. Physics therefore does not determine the outcome. The ball however...'

Tristan stepped forward and took it in his hands in a wildly theatrical gesture that the strange room seemed to encourage. He lifted it back onto the ramp and held it there, on the verge of another fall. 'The ball has no choice. It is never left or right. It is always the direct path.'

Tristan released the ball and it did what it must, returning to the scene of its crime. Its collision with the debris sent up a small cloud of dust. The rector, feigning surprise, left it until the last moment before stepping out of the way.

'And you knew it would do that?' he said.

'Everybody knows it.'

The rector straightened, as he always did at the point of ambush. 'There is the difference between you and me, Tristan. I take nothing for granted. Perhaps, up until this point, the ball has always rolled true, but why dismiss the possibility that all this reflects is a hitherto remarkably consistent personality? How are we to disregard the possibility that at the next trial, having bided its time, the impish thing chooses to surprise us? How can I be so confident that the behaviour of the ball reflects its true nature? What is there in the world that can convince me I am not the subject of an elaborate, spherical conspiracy?'

'What you propose has never been seen,' Tristan said. 'You are right to say that this in itself is not enough to make it impossible. But we live in a world hewn from the past; you taught me as much. That which is true is that which has matched with fidelity our expectations. There is no better definition of truth available to us. I expect the ball to roll, and every time it has. So I say it must roll, and this is all I mean by "must": that it always has, that I can predict with confidence that it will again, and that my prediction has until now never been disappointed.

'This doesn't make it a universal truth,' Tristan continued. 'The exception is always possible. There is no path from observation to universal truth. But neither is there a path to knowledge that does not pass through observation. So we are better to say universal truth is unknowable and content ourselves with this lesser form of knowing. When we speak of truth, this is all we ever mean: established reliability. That is why I do not hold the ball responsible for the crime we witnessed. That is all I mean when I say the ball is essentially different from you and me. I mean that until now, in every time and place it has been observed, the difference has held.'

During interrogations at St Augustine's the boys tried to keep their answers as short as possible. It was a discipline demanded of them and any digression was quickly cauterised. Today, though, the rector waited, as if wishing to hear more. And Tristan took hold of the rope and, with great confidence, fashioned his noose.

'We strive to succeed and mostly we fail, yet we cannot know in advance the manner of our failure; if we did there would be nothing to strive for. The tension between knowledge and intention defines us—it makes us free. It is how I know we make choices, and know we are to be held accountable for these choices. It is why I blame you for lifting the ball, not the ball for destroying the statue.'

Tristan finished, pleased to find the fog clearing from his tired brain. Again the rector smiled.

'Thank you. You have brought us quickly to the point that troubles me most. For, yes, you and I do appear to be morally responsible creatures. You and I do appear to make choices. In our behaviour we are neither random, like a speck of dust buffeted in its cloud, nor predictable, like the ball atop its ramp. Our actions then need further explanation. We are driven by something more: an apparent capacity to pilot our own vessel. Some call it the soul. Only…' he brought his fingers to his chin and leaned forward, as if drawing the words up from some deep dark well, 'only, we are beginning to discover things that, well, they challenge me.

'Tristan, what will follow will not always be pleasant. But knowledge is never easy; it is the fruit of battle, and if our lives are to mean anything we must be prepared for the fight.

'I could say more, but now is not the time. I will let you rest and consider the things we have discussed. You will live here now. The less you know, the more I can be sure our results will not be tainted. This morning has been a promising start. Thank you.'

A short man dressed in a technician's white coat entered the room.

'Tristan, this is Simon. He will show you to your room.'

Tristan felt cheated. Where was the fight he longed to have, even if defeat was certain?

'And if I refuse to comply?' he asked.

'You should have thought of that before you chose to betray us,' the rector replied.

Tristan considered standing his ground, but with every second the gesture became more childish. He banked his remaining dignity and turned.

At first glance his room was most agreeable. It too was painted white. There was a small comfortable bed, more luxurious than anything Tristan had experienced in the dormitories, a chair and, in an adjoining room, a toilet and sink with clear running water. Tristan was exhausted and fell easily into sleep. Only on waking did he discover himself a prisoner.

The room's steady light appeared to glow from the walls. There were no windows and Tristan could find no other source, or detect any shadows. The only door, leading back out into what he remembered as a short dark corridor, was locked. He knocked loudly and waited, but there was no response.

In the steady, white light there was no means of measuring the passing time. One moment Tristan was sure only minutes had elapsed since waking; the next a creeping paranoia convinced him whole days were slipping by unnoticed. From there, it was a small step to imagine he had been left to die. He had been naïve to think a boy who had dared question the wisdom of the Holy Council would be treated in any other way. His hunger grew, fed by the imagined hours. He sat in the chair and counted his pulse as a way of marking time. He studied the tap, the drains and the toilet, seeking a weakness in the room's defences: some crack of natural light or the hint of a draught. He found nothing. He knocked again. He cried. He composed his protests, imagined improbable escapes and tried to ignore his thirst, so that the end would be less protracted.

When Simon finally returned he told Tristan that two days had passed. Tristan could think of no reason to trust him.

Simon led him back to the interrogation room. There was no sign of the bust or the ramp. Only the rector was present, smiling his greeting as if Tristan had been gone only a matter of minutes.

'What are you doing to me?' Tristan demanded.

'It was unpleasant, I imagine,' the rector replied. 'If it is any consolation, it was designed to be that way.'

'How could that be a consolation?' Tristan felt his fury returning. Simon left, closing the door behind him. It was just the two of them again, set in opposition, afloat in the whiteness. The rector spoke quietly, his eyes soft with concern, his voice smooth and reasonable.

'I suppose I meant that if I was to suffer in such a way I would not wish to think my pain was without purpose. You can return to being fed, with a clock in the room and the lights switched off during the hours of darkness, as soon as you like. You have only to ask.'

'I did ask,' Tristan protested. 'I knocked but nobody came. I shouted. I cried out.'

'Yes, unfortunately we needed to acclimatise you first. But now that you see clearly the shape of your suffering, you may ask to end it. Would you like it to end?'

But with the rector nothing was simple.

'Of course I would like it to end.'

'Good.' The rector smiled. 'I would be the same, I am sure. Put out your hands, please.'

Tristan did as he was asked. The rector stooped to pick up a small box that until then had been hidden by his legs. From the box he lifted a kitten. Its soft fur was as white as the room, giving unnatural depth to its wide pleading eyes. The rector passed the trembling creature to Tristan. He felt its puny heart beating out terror's accelerated time.

'All you need to do,' the rector said, 'is break the kitten's neck. Do that and your fast will be broken, your confinement relieved.'

Tristan had killed animals before. It was one of the tasks in the kitchen and no boy, no matter how delicate, was spared the duty. But never a kitten. And never like this. The creature sat powerless in his hands as Tristan stood powerless before the rector, a line of empathy that, irrational though it may have been, could not be denied. It was the twitching nervousness of the face, the expanse of its eyes. And for what? Some tired philosophical abstraction? The rector's amusement?

'I can't,' Tristan said, and the sound of the words echoing in the room made him feel strong and certain. 'It is cruel and pointless and I won't be part of it.'

'Then you will be returned to your room,' the rector said, 'and the conditions will not be altered. Are you sure?'

'I am sure,' Tristan replied, steadfast and proud. 'If that is my punishment, then I shall bear it.'

'Very well, pass me the animal. Thank you. Now look inside the box. There is an envelope. Take it back to your room with you. Do not read the note inside until you are there. We will talk again.'

'When?' Tristan asked. 'How long will you leave me this time?'

'Time is complicated, Tristan,' the rector replied.

His cell was as he had left it. Still without food, Tristan's stomach was beginning to cramp. He lay on the bed, resolving to sleep as much as possible in an attempt to conserve his energy. But first there was the note.

Tristan will be offered release on the condition that he kill the kitten. He will choose not to kill it and so will be returned to the room. He will come to regret his decision.

No time ticked, no shadows moved, no noise penetrated Tristan's empty cell. He felt himself shrinking.

§

Grace gave a dismissive grunt, jolting Tristan from his story.

'That's the problem with you St Augustine's boys,' she said. 'You're all so smart it's made you stupid.'

'What do you mean?'

'It's a simple trick,' she sighed. 'No street child would have fallen for it.'

'It was no trick.'

'He puts one envelope in the box. If you refuse to kill the kitten he gives it to you. If you'd killed it, he would have produced another envelope, perhaps from his pocket, containing the opposite prediction, just as accurate, just as frightening.'

Tristan had reached the same conclusion as soon as the shock had passed. He had not included it in his story for a simple reason. It was wrong.

'I know things you don't know,' he said, regretting at once all that must follow.

'I doubt that,' Grace replied with a calm confidence that recalled the rector.

'You do not know my story,' he said.

'So tell me.'

'You interrupted.'

'Do you think we will die?' she asked.

'We all die eventually.'

'It's the timing that concerns me.'

'It concerned the rector too,' Tristan replied, pulling her back to his tale. He didn't feel strong enough yet to invite death into the conversation.

§

Two more days passed. Tristan spent the time drifting between sleep and stupor. His hunger became muted and his sense of panic less severe. In his lucid moments he thought of the young woman. He imagined her back at the chapel, the candlelight on her face dancing in time to the choir's singing, and he conjured grand dreams of meeting her again. He remembered the body he had sketched for the rector, and it became her body. Such sweet thoughts took the place of sustenance and he rolled easily into sleepy hallucinations.

The next time he stood before the rector, Tristan was determined to give nothing away. Four days without food had weakened his body but strengthened his resolve. Tristan swayed, trying to find his balance. The light bled at the edges of his vision, causing the rector to come into and out of focus.

'You must be hungry,' the rector said.

'There are worse things to be.'

'I always imagined that was the sort of thing people with full stomachs said.'

'I'd rather be hungry than helpless,' Tristan replied.

'The note must have come as a surprise.'

'I am not impressed by a note,' Tristan told him. 'I assume there were others.'

The rector held Tristan's stare and reached into the folds of his gown. He produced another envelope.

'Take this now, Tristan, lest there be any further misunderstanding. I'll not have accusations of trickery. In a moment you may open it. But first I have a question for you.'

Tristan held the envelope in his fingertips, the future in his hands.

'What is your question?'

'The night we caught you coming back through the tunnel after witnessing the passing, who was it you spoke to outside the chapel?'

The rector smiled as Tristan lurched before him.

'Nobody. I talked to nobody.'

'There was a convent girl there,' the rector continued, as if the words had not registered, 'comforting the mothers. Her name is Grace. She is two years older than you. Is there anything you would like to know about her?'

As if the rector could read his very thoughts. Tristan shook the possibility from his head. Someone had followed him, that was all.

'What can I tell you about her, Tristan?' the rector repeated.

Where should he start? Tristan wanted to know what made her laugh, and cry. He wanted to know the smells of her childhood and the rhythm of her breath when she slept.

He wanted to know of the dreams she had never shared and from whom she'd learnt her graceful way of moving. He wanted to know if she had promised herself to God, and, if she had, how Tristan might challenge his maker to a duel. But he asked none of these questions. She did not belong in that barren room. Tristan stared at his feet.

'Very well then, perhaps my question needs refining. Perhaps what you say is true. Perhaps you didn't talk to her. But she talked to you. Repeat her words to me. I am sure you've not forgotten them. Do that and your reward will be food, control of the lighting in your room, the freedom to roam. Think carefully how you answer, for your response is already written. You hold it in your hand. Try not to let this fact unsettle you.'

The rector did nothing to hide his joy, delighting in the guessing game as a child might. Tristan's hunger tightened, but so did his desire to win.

What are you? Three simple words he would never forget, although he did not understand them. Tristan stared at the envelope, as if with sufficient concentration he could see through the paper to the message within. It was simple, surely. The rector would guess at his loyalty to her, and bet on him refusing to answer, just as he had refused to kill the kitten. To beat him, then, meant betraying her. The twin urges collided, unmaking his tired mind.

Tristan looked again at the rector and held his stare, hoping to read some clue there, but the rector's eyes only crinkled with pleasure. *Yes*, they mocked, *but have I already anticipated your calculation?* Suddenly a third possibility presented itself. Tristan dismissed the first option and let a coin tumble inside his head.

Tails. It was decided.

'All right then,' Tristan said. 'You win. She said, "You don't belong here." That was all. She fled before I could say anything in return.'

He delivered the lie without stumbling, holding the rector's unblinking eye.

'That is all I will tell you. You will not get another detail from me. Now where is my food?'

'I will ask for nothing more,' the rector assured him. 'I am not the cheating type. Open the envelope.'

> *Tristan will be asked what the girl said to him. He will answer, but his answer will be a lie.*

Tristan dropped the paper to the floor and bent forward, hands on knees, breathing deeply. The world swam. A droplet of sweat grew too heavy for his forehead and dripped to the floor.

'Don't worry, Tristan, you will be fed. This part of the experiment is over. I will see you when you have eaten.'

§

'I didn't mean to betray you. I thought I could outwit him, but I was a child beating my fists against a giant. I thought then I would never be a match for him.'

Telling it now, the shaking returned, the great echoing

emptiness reverberating across the years.

Tristan felt Grace's impatient wriggling.

'Another simple trick,' she spat.

'I know what you are going to say.'

He wished she wouldn't do this: struggle as he had struggled. He wanted her to be still and listen, that her pain might not be made worse. But she would not, could not. Such was her trajectory.

'How many possibilities are there?' Grace demanded. 'You tell the truth, you lie, you refuse to answer. So only three envelopes are needed. He didn't say how you would lie. He didn't know the details. You have no way of knowing there weren't other boys in other rooms, subject to the same experiments. Perhaps there were six of you, enough to guarantee a hit. How do you know there weren't? How do you know chance is not the author of your story?'

'Do you think I would be telling you this, if it was all I had?'

'You sounded impressed,' she said.

'I was impressed.'

'By a cheap trick.'

'By what followed the trick,' he countered.

'But you didn't know what was to follow. You were stupid from the start.'

A great shiver took possession of Tristan's head, a pain like that caused by an intense burst of coldness, compressing to a point deep beneath his temple. He gagged, but his throat was dry. Again the world was moving in on him. How long was it since he had known anything, since knowing could be relied upon?

'I wish you were right,' he said.

She moved and he felt her cheek rise to his. They lay quietly for a moment, the boy from the experiment and the girl from the chapel. Something like happiness washed over him. The wind had eased and the rain now beat a constant rhythm on the car floor above them. Tristan felt water pooling at his elbow.

'Will you tell me what happened next,' Grace murmured, 'if I promise to keep quiet?'

'Just promise to do your best,' he said. 'The rest is beyond us.'

§

Tristan was given food as promised, along with a clock and control of the lights. Simon delivered the meal and sat beside him while he ate, offering inconsequential conversation. The next morning when Tristan was called back before the rector he felt heavier, more solid in the world, and with this weight came ambition. The envelopes were nothing more than a series of tricks, a test devised by the rector, which Tristan would learn to master. It was expected of him. He expected it of himself.

A desk had been moved into the white room and the rector sat at it, hands clasped behind his neck, stomach denting where it met the polished wood. There was one other chair, and the rector nodded for Tristan to sit.

Between them on the desk sat a finely finished pewter

binary cradle. It rocked slowly to one side and then the other, each oscillation taking the better part of a minute. The grace of the gradual tilting mesmerised Tristan. He had seen a diagram of such a piece in the library, but had not been aware the college owned a working model. When the tilt reached a critical angle a hundred tiny ball bearings rolled out of their holding rut and poured through a delicate confusion of branching passages. The running balls made a sound like the rainstorms Tristan remembered on the tin roof of his childhood home. He observed the way each potential pathway forked and rejoined, like the braids of a river. The balls jostled and rolled their way along the possibilities, like children rushing to play. The paths resolved into seven chutes where the balls collected. A finely set spring then collapsed the chutes, delivering the balls to another holding rut, ready for the next iteration. The rector said nothing as they watched the perpetual stream of crafted chance unfold. Tristan bided his time, knowing the silence would not last.

'Observe any ball, Tristan.' The rector spoke slowly, his voice carefully modulated, his eyes fixed on the boy. 'There is no way of knowing which of the many paths it will take. You can guess, but your guess will be wrong far more often than it is right. And yet, if we view the hundred ball bearings not individually but as a whole unit, we find a curious thing. The more balls we bring into play, the less difficult it becomes to predict their behaviour. For any oscillation the largest number of balls will end up in the centre chute and as we move out towards the extremes we will find fewer and fewer balls. And I can be even more accurate than that. I can predict the ratio of balls in the centre to balls at the ends of any of the other paths. My guesses will not be perfect, but they will be close. They will fall within what you might like to think of as a margin of error. And as we aggregate my guesses over more and more trials, that margin will become smaller and smaller. The future turns scrutable. Look closely.'

The rector reached for the cradle and for a moment stilled its rocking so that the balls paused, ready for release. He traced a path with his finger. 'Imagine a ball set free at the centre. At the first fork it might go left, and at the second fork, left again, and then left at the third. But to go left at each of the six branches requires a degree of unlikelihood we can easily calculate. One half to the power of six, or one chance in sixty-four. So one in sixty-four balls will end up here, on average. On a run of a hundred balls you will see one ball here, or sometimes two, other times none. You will not see nine or ten. That is the law of averages. But while there is only one way of making it to the outside, there are many, many ways to end up in the centre. A left followed by a right perhaps, then another left. Or perhaps two lefts, followed by a right. Chance begins to cancel itself out. Watch, now they run, and see the way this happens: many paths converging into a few. From the chaos emerges pattern.

'You will remember when I showed you the ball on a ramp, you told me the ball had no choice but to smash the bust. You said you knew this from the fact that you were able to predict its behaviour. But now we see there was something wrong with your reasoning. For in the cradle we cannot say the ball has no choice. Indeed the ball has a succession of choices. Left or right, again and again. The individual ball in the cradle, unlike the ball on the ramp, is highly unpredictable. Yet we do not say the balls, forced though they are to make choices, have will. When we observe the balls in the cradle we say their actions are random, that the forces operating on them, though determining, are too complex for us to model. And tacitly we assume this determination to be the antithesis of will.

'But beware the unspoken, Tristan, for quickly it becomes the unexamined. We take will, if we are honest, to be that thing which is not determined; we believe that for it to have any meaning it must spring up within us, separate from the constraints of our physical world. And that, some have always worried, makes free will an impossible thing.'

He watched Tristan carefully as he spoke, always the teacher. Pride kept the pupil's mind on the explanation, wrestling with it, probing it for weakness.

'This brings us to Augustine's paradox,' the rector continued. 'For just as the world of the ball is shaped by physics, we are taught the world of the human is shaped by God. How can there be real will in such a world, when we are subject to His greater plan? Might our free will reduce to nothing more than an illusion—"apparent free will", as the philosophers once liked to call it? Is it not possible that the way we behave is inevitable? After all, we are taught that God knows in advance how we will act. What then is left for us to decide? Are we not mere actors playing our roles? Wouldn't that process—if the causal factors were complex enough for us to lose sight of their individual components and see only the broader effects—feel just like free will? Think again of a single ball in the cradle. What if it had developed a consciousness sophisticated enough to explain each random path it took in terms of choices and motivations it had invented. Would it not be tempted to believe it was free, even though you and I can stand above it and see a different truth, just as God stands above us? Isn't there also a temptation for us to begin to believe we possess a level of control that in fact does not exist? And is this belief not itself a form of blasphemy? What do you think, Tristan? I am interested in your answer.'

'It would be as blasphemous of me to consider that I had solved the paradox,' Tristan replied.

'Very well, let me release you from your sense of propriety. I take it you are familiar with the heathen philosophers. What is it they say on the matter?' The rector straightened his back and Tristan heard vertebrae clicking into place. He knew he was being manipulated. This topic was familiar territory; he could range over it with a fluidity no other boy had ever matched, and because of this he couldn't resist. He would answer, and with every word he would trade away a little of his soul.

'The heathen philosophers would say you have already given the answer. If there is no way of knowing the difference between being free and simply feeling as if we are free, then may this not be a way of saying the difference is ill defined? The problem of free will is not one of substance, but rather one of definition. You may say the way we behave is the way we were always going to behave, that faced with exactly the same circumstances we would behave the same way again. Yet, to be faced with the same circumstances, down to the smallest detail, is to find oneself not just at the same place, but also in the same time. And if this is the requirement then our repeated experiment contains no repetition at all; it is simply the same event restated. We are left with the proposition "what happens happens", a truism which adds nothing to our understanding. The problem of free will is seductive only because it is poorly framed. This at least is what the heathen philosophers might argue.'

The rector leaned forward in his chair, bringing his great hands together with a delighted clap.

'Yes, yes, this is precisely what they say. And yet, there is a flaw in the clever argument. What is it, Tristan? Tell me.'

Committed to the case, Tristan had no choice but to proceed, even as the trap became suddenly clear—he was a prisoner forced to announce the terms of his own execution.

'Augustine struggled with the definition of time. He knew that to understand time is to understand existence. I do not claim to have reached such a point, nor do I ever hope to, but in the noble attempts of our forebears we can find important clues. It is true, as they say, that we cannot move back through time to repeat an experiment, but we can move forward in time to anticipate one. This is the luxury afforded us by our imagination. We alone are the creature who meets the future prepared: *Homo predictus*. And if we can predict the behaviour of a man in advance,' Tristan conceded, 'the distinction between real and apparent free will is no longer an abstraction. We can define the free man as one whose actions remain inscrutable, whereas the man who is only apparently free can in principle have his every move predicted. An experiment presents itself to those who argue against the will.'

'Yes, it does!' the rector agreed. 'For will then becomes defined as the ability to confound expectations. If I can tell you in advance what you will do, even before you decide to do it, then I have established your will as illusion. And that is why you fit our experiment so well. You have shown yourself to be most wilful. And clever and resourceful. And now you have the last ingredient: knowledge. You know what the experiment is for, and so it cannot be said that you were tricked into your actions.'

'But what if I attempt to subvert the experiment?' Tristan asked. 'What if I deliberately behave in ways that are out of character and unpredictable?'

'But this is exactly what you must do,' the rector exclaimed, showing surprise that this point had not been anticipated. Or perhaps only apparent surprise, for wherever Tristan moved he found the rector already there, pushing back. 'If you do not attempt to beat the experiment it has no meaning. Habit is easily predicted; no one has ever claimed it isn't. It is the intentional, tactical, motivated mind we seek to expose. That is the prize.'

'But my knowledge is not perfect,' Tristan objected. 'I know the what of the experiment but not the why. Do you really want to see me fail? Would that not mean the death of responsibility, the slaying of the soul?'

The rector hesitated, his features for a moment dissolving into uncertainty, but he composed himself again before Tristan could be sure.

'I want you to try to beat the game; that is all you need to know.'

It was no answer at all, and Tristan sensed a weakness in his opponent.

'But your experiment is already compromised. I am here against my will, undertaking the experiment only as punishment for a transgression.'

'And so you wish to destroy the experiment?' the rector asked.

'Why shouldn't I?'

'Then you have not been listening. I want you to attempt to destroy it. That is the point. You must choose the behaviour that best suits your goal. My job is to anticipate it.'

'You will fail,' Tristan said, his body growing tall with certainty. 'You cannot know my mind. I do not even know it myself.'

The rector didn't flinch. 'Pick a number,' he said. 'A number between one and ten. Don't tell me what it is. Here, write it on this paper; turn away, don't let me see what you have chosen.'

Tristan took the paper and turned. At once he felt his mind locking up, as if some grit had got amongst the cogs. It was the scrutiny: his brain turned shy. *Close your eyes and take the first number you think of,* he told himself, and yet trying made the simple task of thinking of a number impossible. With deliberate thought all ten presented themselves. He cursed his ineptitude and the fact the rector could read his struggle in the time that had passed. Seven. Seven insisted itself on him, but it was too obvious. Didn't everybody choose seven? Impulsively he scribbled a three, folding the paper over before turning as calmly as he could to his challenger.

The rector showed no hesitation. 'You wrote three,' he said, not even glancing at the paper. 'Most people, when they are asked, think of seven. And when they are trying to avoid being anticipated they deliberately reject their first thought. You are a tidy person, you enjoy symmetry; the jump from seven to three is a reflection about five. It feels like the least obvious attempt to avoid the obvious. And yet…am I right?'

He took the paper and unfolded it. There was no satisfaction on his face, as if this victory was too small to mark.

'I guessed, Tristan. I got lucky. This is not how we will proceed. But there is a point to be made. We are creatures of instinct, capable of learning, it is true; but that is no more than the process of writing a new instinct over an old one. We feel rational only because of our extraordinary capacity for attributing motivation to actions as they unfold. We are not the players in our lives; we are the commentators. Or such is my claim and you will be my evidence. You have no will. Even your desire to subvert your instincts is based on a deeper pattern of instinctive behaviour, harder to read but not, I contend, impossible.'

'You are wrong.'

'Perhaps,' the rector conceded. 'Either way we shall find out. Look again at the cradle. All is pattern, don't you see?

'You and I are made of molecules, Tristan. Our brains

possess only the unity we bestow upon them as a matter of convenience. Thought is not a linear process overseen by some ghostly homunculus; it is an electrochemical storm, a wild competition between memories and associations from which emerges a winner called action. We misname it decision. The illusion provides us great comfort. The heathens like to believe they have outgrown the need for myths, but here is the one myth even they cannot do without: the myth of self.

'For a long time people thought that predicting the mind was impossible. But look again at the cradle. From the random emerges the predictable; in the behaviour of the aggregate, the individual can be read. Consider not the ball; the ball is not the prize. Consider instead the collection of balls. We are accurate in our predictions not because we understand the physics of individual collisions, but precisely because we ignore them.

'This test means nothing if you do not fight it. Do not lose your great capacity for doubt, do not stop probing my tests for their weaknesses. You must make me prove it to you.'

The rector stood and walked ceremoniously around the table. He paused before Tristan and placed a hand on each cheek, leaned forward and kissed his forehead.

'Make it your business to defeat me.'

'I already was,' Tristan hissed at him. It was true. Once he had loved this man; in less than a week he had learnt to hate him.

The rector gave an approving nod. 'We will now conduct tests and take measurements; the trials we have put you through so far have been the games of children. Any astute observer might easily have guessed your path. You will make your confession in your room each evening, for I cannot have anyone claiming my work was made easy by the damaged state of your soul. You will have many questions and you must always feel free to ask them. I will not see you again until the final challenge. Good luck, Tristan. I wish you well.'

Tristan stood slowly, hopeful that the mess inside his head would soon resolve itself, but no coherent thought emerged, and he walked unsteadily to his room.

That night a priest came to Tristan's room to hear his confession. He was a small man, neither young nor old, lined but not sagging, his grey hair just long enough to stand in a small gesture of defiance. He laid out the contrition map and unfolded a stand, placing the holy icon on it. Tristan knelt before the image as he had so many times before. Tonight, though, its hues appeared deeper, more vibrant, and in the careful gaze of the three founders Tristan fancied there was a message just for him, if only he could learn to read it. He gazed on Plato's gleaming locks, caught in the last rays of sunlight, and the proud gold working of the throne on which he sat. He looked down at the crimson robes of the two prophets standing one on either side of the philosopher, Jesus and Augustine, each staring confidently beyond the dimensions of the painting, as if they too could read the future.

The same priest returned each night for the next two years. He spoke the words prescribed by the ritual, and listened attentively as Tristan gave the full account of his weaknesses. He did not share his name, and never lingered after the ceremony or gave any hint he was interested in conversation.

Tristan didn't mind—he had Simon for company when he needed it, and most days he didn't. The hours were full: each morning he was taken to a laboratory and subjected to testing. People interviewed him, poring over the smallest scraps of his memory like beggars gleaning at a dump site. Others took measurements. They shone lights into his eyes and attached wires to his scalp and chest. They tested his reflexes, asked him to invent stories or tell lies, and took his temperature. They showed him pictures and asked him what he saw. They submerged him in water, recording his physical responses as the panic took hold. They gave him long lists of words to memorise and made him recite them while they tried to distract him. They extracted blood and opinions, frightened him and lied to him and recorded his hormone levels and neural images.

Tristan complied. He was determined to beat the rector, but not through trickery. He had no shortage of motivation. He was competitive by nature: his instinct to rise to any challenge had propelled his unlikely journey from the workers' quarter to the secret laboratory. Then there was the matter of time. Like thousands of prisoners before him, he sought to keep himself busy, to blunt the edge of his incarceration with routine and activity. And, being on the cusp of manhood, he was easy prey to fantasies of heroism. To beat the rector, he dimly hoped, would be to strike a blow for all that was good and worthy. It was to take the side of two young women and make amends for his cowardice. Most of all, though, Tristan was motivated by fear. To lose this challenge would be to lose his self.

He had been through the arguments at the college, but they had retained an abstract quality. They were just points to be made and unmade, to be wrapped in eloquence or hurled as weapons. Somehow they never managed to leak into the life he lived. No matter how vehemently he argued otherwise, Tristan never lost his faith that it was he who was doing the arguing. He, this soulful self, was choosing when to attack and when to block, when to yield and when to divert. His will was real, and it was free. It made no more sense to doubt this than to doubt sense itself. Even within his small room he could live a life woven from choices. He could choose when to walk, when to pause, when to turn, when to sit, even when to breathe. Didn't he choose each night which thoughts to confess to the priest and which to keep secret?

So Tristan knew he could not lose, and yet at the same time he understood victory wasn't certain. The rector was a formidable opponent. Not even in his proudest moments had Tristan ever believed he might be a match for him. He was left with no choice but to grow stronger, shake his thoughts free of the easy ruts of habit and instinct. He dwelt on the number he had been asked to pick. The rector was right: three was the obvious choice. But how to make the unobvious choice? That became the question, the obsession.

Tristan reasoned that if he could come to recognise the patterns of a forming decision, he could also learn to intervene before the intention became the deed. This simple plan buoyed him, and gave shape to the hours he spent alone. Each evening after his confession was heard, he turned to the meditation he had practised at the college.

In those days the aim had been to leave the self behind; now Tristan was interested in the boundary between knowing and being, where he might experience the whirring of his mind from the outsider's perspective. Initially his efforts were fruitless. Each time Tristan thought he was getting close his awareness grew too heavy and collapsed the meditative state. In the third month his tenacity was rewarded. He received the first hints of the machinery behind the screen. A simple decision, say to sit in a chair or turn over a pillow, did not arise from nothingness. Each time the pattern was the same. First there came the jostling: a competing choir of choices, a fuzzy noise of possibility so brief that only a trained mind would notice it. The resolution then emerged like a sudden tilting, every new thought sliding down the same slope, pulled there by the increasing gravity of a decision. It was in that instant, Tristan saw, that the other possibilities were written out of existence. The mind closed over them as water closes over when a rock is removed from a stream.

The trick was to look away at precisely the point that the decision tumbled into place. It began with a cup of water. Tristan was feeling thirsty and automatically filled a cup with water. He realised at once that an experiment presented itself and began to meditate. He closed his eyes and made a mantra of the two alternatives. *Drink, pour out the water. Drink, pour out the water…*He relaxed and let the two paths cycle through his mind. Soon the familiar loosening began, as if somewhere within his head the tension was being released. The hum grew stronger, and shards of impulse pierced his unconsciousness. He slowed his breathing and the contradictory instructions sped to a flicker: *drink, pour out the water, drink...*

As he departed his mind he felt the decision carrying on without him, tilting in favour of discarding the water. The tipping point was reached and Tristan was aware of his hand reaching down to the cup. In an instant he seized control, dropping to his knees and pouring the water down his throat before a drop could be spilt. He fell to the floor as a madman might, clutching the empty cup to his heart and laughing out loud at the strangeness of his new power.

There was no telling how long the road would be between the first step and mastery. Subsequent attempts showed that timing was everything. Move too soon and the decision would evaporate before Tristan could be sure he had identified it. Leave it too late and awareness came on only after the act itself was completed. The window was small, if it existed at all. In his weaker moments he began to believe he had invented his first victory. Even then, though, there was one thing that could console him, a small indulgence he allowed himself before falling asleep.

Each night as his thoughts turned lazy she would return to him, painted in the unworldly colours of an oncoming dream. The voices of the choir became more heavenly with each replaying, and her face became more beautiful. He whispered to her, feverish words of desire, and she whispered back her delight, warming him to slumber. He remembered and he imagined, letting his mind roam where it would, but with his fists clenched by his side. All was will. All was training.

§

Tristan had reached the point where he might speak his heart.

'There was never a time I did not think of you. There was never a time I stopped loving you.'

'Not me,' Grace countered. 'Your idea of me.'

'It's all we ever have,' Tristan replied, thinking of how much he would have once given to lie this close to her.

'You hadn't even spoken to me.'

'I am speaking to you now.'

'Is it a disappointment?'

'The circumstance,' Tristan conceded, 'but not the sensation.'

So weakened was he by his confession that he almost broke his promise to himself. He almost told her. But not yet. Too many events sat between that place and this.

'I saw you again, you know,' Tristan said. 'I watched you.'

'So you beat the rector?'

'No one beats the rector.'

'But you got out,' Grace said.

'I got lucky.'

'I thought you had a plan.'

'Yes,' Tristan said. 'But my plan was flawed.'

'Can I guess at it?' she asked.

Tristan was surprised by her enthusiasm. She had been so quiet during his story that he feared he had bored her with his philosophy, or worse. Now he could hear her fighting to master her breathing, the heavy aspiration easily mistaken for excitement.

'If you intended to do the opposite of whatever your brain decided, and the rector did find a way of anticipating your decisions, it would be a small adjustment for him to adapt to your strategy.'

Tristan was embarrassed by how easily she had exposed his naïveté.

'I thought, when there was more than one alternative, I could lose him. But instead I lost myself. Each decision required another, and there was no way of ending the regress.'

'So what did you do?'

'I gave up.'

§

And in giving up, Tristan discovered the art of looking away. It was a sort of abdication of responsibility, a blind blundering into the path of a decision. When it happened, the oddest events followed. He would come to his senses to find himself sitting on the floor scratching at a toe that wasn't itching, or balancing a knife on the end of his nose, or fashioning his bed sheet into a ridiculous robe. Not once could he explain to himself how the decision had been arrived at, and this, he was sure, would become his trump. If he did not know why he did these things, if they occurred without reason or motivation, then the rector could never predict them. Tristan would defeat him.

When finally he was summoned to the rector again, he approached his teacher with confidence.

In two years Tristan had changed considerably. They'd allowed him a mirror and he knew he had taken on the look of a young man. He had grown tall and his shoulders had broadened. Each morning now he made use of the shaving equipment provided. The rector must have noticed all these things but he gave no sign of it. The white room was as it always had been, and the rector too, standing in the middle of it, appeared exempt from the chiselling of time. He held his ground with unnatural stillness, his eyes watching the young man without so much as a flicker.

Beside the rector was a pile of wooden puzzle pieces, cut with various notches so that they could be locked together to form a larger shape. Tristan was familiar with such sets from St Augustine's, where they had been used in logic classes. These ones differed in scale: the shortest of the twenty parts was as long as his arm. According to a diagram affixed to the far wall the pieces would form the shape of a crucifix, one that, by Tristan's calculations, would be roughly full size.

'Welcome, Tristan.'

Tristan looked deep into the rector's eyes while in his head he ran backwards through the alphabet, so that any nervousness might be distracted out of existence. The rector returned his gaze, and their eyes remained locked. When the rector blinked first Tristan felt a thrill buzz through him.

'Are you ready to be defeated?' Tristan challenged.

'That is something I will never be ready for, Tristan,' the rector answered. 'Are you?'

'I haven't even contemplated it.'

'I am told the testing has gone very well, Tristan; you have been a most willing subject. Thank you.' The rector spoke with his usual measured clarity. Tristan scanned the room for signs of danger. He would not be lured into complacency.

'Now we are ready to move to the next stage in the experiment. As I told you two years ago, the simple tricks of our early trial are not sufficient to convince the doubters of the will's constraints. Nor should they be. In those cases you were limited to binary choices; however, the world in which we move is far more chaotic. It is my intention to establish, to the satisfaction of those who would attack me, that in the interactions between independently motivated players a trajectory can still be mapped in advance. This is the end of your time with us, and how you act today will see my purpose either realised or thwarted. In a moment I will introduce you to your two competitors.'

Tristan gave an involuntary start. The rector pretended not to have noticed. Competitors? Tristan breathed deeply and repeated to himself his mantra. *Leave the scene. Let the future unfold without you.*

'Behind the far wall,' the rector continued, 'there are three members of the Holy Council. They have come to observe the experiment. You cannot see them.'

Immediately Tristan's mind returned to his room, its walls an identical sheen. Had he been watched all this time? How close had they stood, he wondered, while he lay sleeping? Had they watched his meditations? Of course they had. A shiver ran through him and again he attempted to shrug it off. *Leave the scene. Let the future unfold without you...*

'Each of our observers holds a description of the game that is about to be played, the decisions you'll make and the outcome. I have anticipated the way you will play, the decisions you will make. An identical description can be found in this envelope, which I would ask you to put in the pouch of your robe. At the conclusion of the game you may also read this description. I want you to know what has happened to you.' He passed the envelope to Tristan.

An idea rose unbidden. *Look inside the envelope. Do it now and you have won.* So simple, so tempting.

'I can do whatever I want to subvert the game?' Tristan asked.

'It is what I have asked of you.'

It was too simple.

'But be careful, Tristan. All has been anticipated.'

Either the note said *You will look inside the envelope* or it didn't. There was only one way of losing this game, and there were a thousand ways of winning. Looking would reduce those odds to a binary choice. It would be a foolish move. And yet they knew that.

Do not think of the envelope. He wants you to think of the envelope. He wants it to distract you. Ignore the envelope.

Tristan folded the envelope once and slipped it into the pouch. The rector smiled without effort, confident, certain. Tristan's determination to destroy that calm burned brighter than it ever had.

'Excellent.' The rector nodded, as if in agreement with some unspoken point. 'In a moment two boys will enter the room. Each, as you will see, is about your age and size. They are children of the night, soulless ones who have endured a life of struggle. Today they play for the ultimate prize, for the winner of the game will be offered the freedom of the City, an unprecedented opportunity to be baptised and live within our walls. So you see they will not lack motivation. To them this is a matter of life and death. The task is a simple one: the three of you will work together to solve the puzzle, and whichever of you slots the last piece into place will be declared the winner. There is no second place.'

'Then I have nothing to play for,' Tristan noted. 'I am already baptised.'

'Yes,' the rector agreed. 'Your prize is different. If you win today, Tristan, we will take you to Grace.'

Tristan's head was reeling. He hadn't mentioned her again: not in the interviews, the tests, not even alone in his room. Yet they knew.

Leave the scene. Leave the scene.

But the scene was boundless. It followed him; it lived inside his head.

Leave the scene.

'I see you remember her. Good. Insert the final piece and we will take you to the girl. You will have all the money you need to make a new life, papers, and a new name to wear.'

It was perfect, the trap they had set for him. He saw it instantly. Everything he had done to prepare had been based on a single premise: that nothing was more important to him that defeating the rector. And now he saw it wasn't true. It had never been true. There had always been her.

'What are the rules of this game?' Tristan managed to ask.

'There are no rules,' the rector answered. 'But don't worry; they won't kill you.'

'You can't know that,' Tristan countered.

'It is written in the envelope, Tristan.' The rector stepped slowly backwards. 'It is written in the envelope.'

When the rector reached the wall a hidden door slid open. In the darkened room beyond, Tristan caught a shadowed glimpse of the observers from the Holy Council. Then came a sound from behind, the sort of snuffling you might expect from a large animal sniffing at the air.

Tristan turned to see two boys standing one on either side of the door. They studied him. The one on the left was short and thickset, his head a mass of red curls. His feet were widely planted as if he were expecting some great storm to break over him. He looked from Tristan to the puzzle pieces then back again. Tristan turned to his other opponent: a taller boy, slender, bouncing on his feet like an athlete at the starting line. The second boy grinned. 'You ready for this?' he asked. 'I'm Louis; this is Harry.'

'I'm not Harry,' the redhead growled.

'Well, you look like a Harry,' Louis replied. He turned back to Tristan. 'What shall we call you?'

'Tristan.' The stranger's friendliness undid him, and Tristan relaxed when he should have been watching. The shorter boy moved quickly, his shoulder finding Tristan's stomach and dropping him winded to the floor. His opponent dispatched, the redhead scrambled at the pieces, attempting to secure a pile for himself. Tristan rolled on the floor to find Louis standing above him, still grinning as if this was nothing more than a game in the schoolyard. Louis offered a bony hand and pulled Tristan to his feet. Tristan winced at the pain in his gut and bent double to recover his breath.

'No rules,' Louis reminded him. 'You'll need to be quicker than that. Come on. Do you know how to solve the puzzle?'

Harry was already jamming pieces together, experimenting with random combinations. This wasn't right. This wasn't how it was meant to be. The movement, the urgency, the danger: they crowded in, pinning Tristan to his thoughts. He tried to pull free, but Louis stood close, impossible to ignore.

'I have seen puzzles like it,' Tristan said.

'All right, well then, there is hope for all of us. Oi, Harry, you oaf, you can't keep all the pieces!'

Louis strolled confidently towards the pile. Harry sprang at him, snarling as he grabbed the taller boy's throat, but Louis remained perfectly calm, simply flicking his long foot at Harry's groin. Harry fell to the ground, howling. Louis retrieved the pieces and returned them to the central pile. He circled, studying them closely.

Tristan watched the two boys, one moving with easy charm, the other still snorting as he regained his feet. He tried to stand back, to observe from a greater distance, but his mind would not let go of the room. The rector would have chosen the two boys carefully, anticipating the nature of their clash. He would have known how easily Tristan would solve the puzzle, and how poorly the attendant violence would suit him… What then was written in the envelope Tristan carried in his pouch? But no, there was no envelope, there was no room.

Leave the scene. Let the future unfold without you.

But she was there now, expanding inside his head, squeezing him back into the room.

While Tristan stood aside the others paid him no attention. He breathed deeply and focused on the point of nothingness he had created behind his forehead. He imagined it as a light, pulsing with perfect regularity. He listened to the murmuring of his competing thoughts. Possibilities were swarming, seeking a foothold, each working to lodge its claim. A faint vibration, something like the rasping of metal on wood, resolved into a call to inaction. *Sit the game out*, the pattern urged. *Do nothing; confound them.* The possibility rose then fell away. A deeper, thicker drive hummed beneath the clamour, marshalling its forces. *Win her*, it ordered. *Whatever it takes, win her.* From there a new thought grew, high-pitched and insistent. *They cannot solve this thing without you*, it counselled, *but they don't know it yet. Sit tight. Let them battle. Let them tire themselves out.* As this last thought grew louder the other swirling candidates meekly disassembled, lending weight so quickly to the emerging winner that the naïve mind might have believed it had willed it.

As the decision threatened to settle, Tristan forced himself to look away. With no mind to attach itself to, the impulse fragmented, each connection fizzing and spluttering back to unbeing. Tristan smiled. He did not care if the observers saw him do it. He surged with new power.

'Keep Harry at bay,' Tristan called to Louis, 'and I will complete the puzzle for you. You can have the final piece.

Victory is yours if you can subdue him.'

Louis looked up, immediately suspicious.

'Why should I trust you?' Louis asked. Tristan kept a wary eye on Harry, who had begun circling them both on all fours, as comfortable in the gait as any animal.

'Take this.' Tristan offered him a piece of the puzzle. 'I cannot complete the puzzle without it. And use it as a weapon if I attempt to cross you.'

Louis hesitated, tempted. 'If you are lying to me I will kill you.'

'It is what I expect,' Tristan replied. Louis nodded and took the piece. He stood guard while Tristan set to work on the puzzle. Tristan allowed himself a smile as he imagined the rector slumped in defeat behind the glass while the members of the Holy Council checked their scripts and demanded an explanation.

The puzzle was not difficult and within minutes Tristan was making progress. In the background the children of the night stalked each other, Louis always between Harry and the puzzle.

Harry however was no fool. He seemed to know his best chance lay in unsettling his opponents. He began running around the outside of the room at startling velocity, his jaw flapping as he howled like a wolf. Louis swivelled, attempting to track Harry's crazed trajectory. Tristan tried to ignore the noise and concentrate on the puzzle. He was close to finishing, but the terrible sound panicked him and the heavy pieces began to jam. He felt his arms tiring. The howling grew louder and Louis began to shout over it. 'Back! Back!

Back!' he screamed, as if warding off a wild animal. And then, suddenly, 'Tristan, watch out!'

Harry charged. Tristan sprang clear just in time and his adversary crashed into the almost completed crucifix, propelling it into the wall. Harry pounced on a loose piece of wood, all he needed to remain in the game. Tristan was closer than Louis and instinct propelled him forward. He threw himself on top of the boy and clung to his back for dear life, panicked blood surging through his veins. There was nothing now— no room, no competition, no rector, no Grace—only this moment, and the desperate desire to survive into the next.

Tristan had not lived his life in the wastelands and could not conceive of their brutality. Louis ran forward swinging his puzzle piece as a club, aiming it at the side of Harry's head. The force took Harry sideways and knocked Tristan from his back. Tristan could not tell if the blow had killed him or only knocked him cold. Blood pooled beneath Harry's face, set now in pained bewilderment.

'No rules,' Louis panted. The tall boy's fingers trembled at his side, not with regret, Tristan guessed, but with the afterwash of adrenalin.

Louis looked at Tristan, as if expecting the game to change now. He nodded for Tristan to continue with the puzzle, but Tristan didn't move. In the settling silence a new doubt was taking hold of him. He had followed his own rules, subverted his instincts, but, now the path was clear to him, it felt predictable. Wouldn't the rector have known Tristan's sheltered life had not prepared him for the brutality of the children of the night? What then was more foreseeable than

Tristan putting physical safety ahead of the game, as he now intended to do? Hadn't the rector had him followed to the church that night? They must have seen that he had been too frightened to speak. Faced with love he had yielded to fear. Wasn't it obvious he would do so again?

Tristan remembered the number test and pushed back at the temptation to second-guess. But it was too late: the seeds of doubt gathered quickly into clouds. Tristan moved to the broken puzzle and crouched, ready to engage. His hands became clumsy as his thoughts turned inward, seeking out their motivation. He peered deep, peeling back layer after layer of contrivance. But all he found were more layers. Layers all the way down.

A sudden emptiness tugged at him with a weight denser than sadness. He groped about for the frayed edges of his will and found only her, the young woman, sitting calm in the centre of the storm. *Why do you even want to defeat him? Why would you care? I am here. Come to me.*

The crucifix was almost finished. Tristan made a final adjustment and moved to the other side of the pile, ready to position the penultimate piece. He felt Louis's eyes on him, watchful and certain. It was easy for Louis. His purpose was unshakeable. The piece slid easily into place; the cross was solid now. Tristan stood back and pointed to the place where the last piece would slot.

'Thank you,' Louis said simply. He moved warily to the puzzle.

Tristan closed his eyes but the room pressed closer still. *Leave the scene. Let the future unfold without you.*

No, I am here. Come to me.

Louis leaned in, his hands on the piece. Tristan watched, waited…

He felt his body lurch forward. His shoulder found the small of Louis' back. The boy attempted to swivel but he was already falling. Tristan felt fingers scrabbling for his eyes. He turned from their grasp, reaching for the last piece of the puzzle. A bony thumb found a socket and Tristan's head lit up with pain. But his hands had already found the wood and the impulse was past reversing.

Tristan slid the last piece into place.

He threw his defeated opponent from his back and sprang to his feet, expecting Louis to come for him now and punish him for his betrayal. Louis's eyes were empty. He shrugged and tried to smile.

'Well played,' he whispered.

Tristan felt a great rush of regret. 'I am sorry. I too was playing for my soul.'

Tristan turned to face the back wall, no longer fooled by its blankness. He waited for the verdict. It seemed impossible that they had got to this point before him. Or impossible for anyone but the rector. Triumph flattened to anticipation, and then concern. *It doesn't matter*, her voice whispered. But it did. It mattered. Tristan was shaking.

They emerged in single file, three venerable gentlemen dressed in the purple robes of the Holy Council. They walked across the room and Tristan saw in their dazed faces that he had defeated them. Two victories then, sweeter still. One of the men stopped to contemplate the blood at Harry's head. Another ran a mottled hand across the completed puzzle, as if to confirm this wasn't a dream. None of the three spoke a word. Tristan made no effort to hide his joy. He skipped from one man to the next as a child might, to look more closely on their anguish. Not one met his eye.

They departed without speaking and it was only then that Tristan realised the rector hadn't emerged. That was unfair. Tristan had earned the right to be congratulated.

'Come on!' Tristan shouted to the gap in the wall. 'What are you waiting for? Did you really think you would win?'

There was no response. Tristan walked to the small observation room and found it empty. He felt the same. Why wouldn't he show himself?

'The prize!' he shouted to the empty space. 'You promised me the girl. Where is my prize?'

Still there was no reply.

Tristan remembered the envelope. He would wait here; someone would come eventually. Simon probably. He would know where to find the rector. In the meantime Tristan would read the prediction, see where the great man had made his mistake:

> *At first Tristan will struggle with the violence of the game. He will step aside, in order to stay clear of his own instincts. Tristan will offer Louis a deal, believing this will foil our predictions. He will offer to let Louis slot*

the last piece into place if he in turn can keep Harry out of the game. But Tristan will be shaken by the violence of the competition and this will break his resolve. Strong emotions will bring the girl back into play. He will forsake the game for the girl. At the last moment he will betray Louis, and claim the prize for himself.

Tristan read the words through three times, each time grasping only snatches of their meaning. The greater picture refused to form. He didn't understand. He had seen the men of the Holy Council. They had walked with the heavy footsteps of the defeated. And yet here he read the opposite. He slumped to the floor.

'What is wrong?' Louis asked.

'I don't understand.'

The door opened and Simon entered.

'Where is he?' Tristan demanded. 'Where is the rector?'

'On his way.'

Simon helped a groggy Harry to his feet and escorted him from the room. Louis followed without looking back. As the door clicked shut behind them, the rector announced his presence with a cough, and Tristan turned to him.

The rector walked forward and offered his hand. Tristan refused to take it, standing unassisted. He looked to the ground. Bile rose within him.

'You tried.' The rector spoke gently, a doctor delivering a terminal diagnosis. 'You tried your best. They saw that. They cannot argue otherwise.'

Tristan brought his hands to his ears. He would not

hear this. It was not possible.

'No, I have beaten them,' he cried. 'I saw their faces.'

It was all he had to offer, a child's petulance. The rector looked at him with concern, and Tristan knew what would come next. A question. Always there was a question.

'Do you think defeating me and defeating the Holy Council are the same thing?'

Tristan's thoughts turned slippery, a feeling he had all but forgotten. His mind opened just a fraction and understanding slid into place.

'They are the opposite things?' Tristan said.

'Yes.'

There was a solemnity about the rector now: the teacher returning to his sacred task.

'What you proposed was heresy,' Tristan continued. Understanding is never complete: one thought demands another.

'Of course it is heresy. To have a choice is to have a soul, is this not so?'

'We have been taught so,' Tristan answered.

'But what must we do with all we have been taught?' the rector probed. There was only one interrogation and it never ended.

'Question it.'

'And what first led you to question all we had taught you?'

Tristan's answer was honest and unguarded. There was no competition now, no enemy.

'The girl you made me draw. You said she had no soul.'

'She is a child of the night. It is doctrine that they are

beyond salvation, so why would you question it? What did you see that sparked your doubt?'

Tristan considered his question, the pupil as eager as his teacher to reach their destination.

'Only my instinct. I saw her suffering. I felt it.'

The rector smiled and an old feeling returned to Tristan, the glow that came from pleasing the teacher.

'Ten years ago a series of secret experiments were carried out, crude things in my opinion. We assembled a group of children of the night and showed that under certain circumstances we were able to predict their behaviour well in advance of the children believing they had made any choices.

'In the most telling example we used electrical impulses to guide them through simple mazes. Unaware of these external signals, the children created elaborate stories to explain the paths they had taken. We found we could move them quickly to the maze's heart or trap them in hopeless circles, and either way the children would explain in detail the invented causes of their success or failure.

'This was taken to the Holy Council, which took it as final evidence that the people of the night were nothing more than automatons, trundling through life dressing their trajectories in *post hoc* narrative. The council embraced the finding, for it appeared to support the Doctrine of the Soulless. It was reasonable to conclude that the people of the night, having no will, possessed no souls. Science had given support to lumbering prejudices. This is what believers do: ask only those questions that cannot hurt them.

'Of course there were voices of dissent. Ours is a

community well trained in logic, and the experiment was clearly flawed. I am sure you can tell me why.'

Tristan nodded. It wasn't difficult. 'There were two mistakes. The first was in the leap from the specific to the general. To show that in a particular circumstance will can be an illusion does not establish that the same is true in every circumstance. It is well known that by creating the right conditions of light and line our eyes can be deceived, but no one uses this to imply that all we see is false. We cannot assume that because the children did not notice the absence of will in this case, that the will is always absent in them.'

'And the other mistake?' the rector asked.

'There was no control,' Tristan continued, sensing at once the gap into which he had been thrown. 'Even if they could establish the absence of will in children of the night, it still falls upon them to show that under the same circumstance those possessing souls do not suffer the same reduction.'

The rector nodded his approval, turning to pace in his theatrical manner. He stopped suddenly, as if puzzled by his thoughts.

'If you are right, then the Holy Council, made up as you know of our deepest and most respected thinkers, was quite wrong. How could it be that you have out-thought our finest minds? Is not what you are suggesting foolish arrogance?'

'It may well be,' Tristan said, hearing in his answers thoughts he barely knew were forming. 'But we all have blind spots, and perhaps it is the role of the arrogant to ensure that we are not all looking in the same direction.'

The rector laughed, a deep and gratifying boom that warmed the boy.

'Other arrogant minds approached me,' the rector said, and the satisfaction in his voice rang clear. 'They also believed the council's enthusiasm stemmed not from evidence but from doctrine. Together we devised a further experiment, one that could serve as the control. We presented it to the council for their approval. They raised no objections, for dogma had made them blind. They fully expected to see me fail today, Tristan. They found it inconceivable that a young man like yourself, baptised and schooled in theology, could be reduced to an automaton.'

He gazed down his long nose at Tristan as one might look at the first fruit of a well-tended orchard.

'I am glad we found you, Tristan. You have done more good than you can imagine.'

'You didn't find me,' Tristan reminded him. 'Circumstance delivered me to you. I chose to defy the church. I presented you with the opportunity to punish me.'

The rector's eyes clouded with sadness, an emotion so ill suited to his features that his face became that of a stranger.

'You see how stubborn our beliefs are, Tristan? After all of this, you still believe in choices. I brought you to the naked girl because I knew how it would pain you. I provoked your rebellion and sent Brother Kevin to lead you further. It was important you thought that you were being punished. It was important you saw me as your enemy. I needed to be able to convince the council you wished for nothing more than my defeat.'

'I wished for the girl at the church more,' Tristan reminded him. 'Or was she a lie too? Did you pay her to act that way?'

'No, Grace came as a surprise. But not one I couldn't utilise.'

'So she's real?'

'Yes.'

'And you can take me to her?'

'You will have your prize.'

It should have been all that mattered. He would see her again, and this time he would not hesitate. This experiment would fade to a dream in his memory. It should have been that simple. And yet anger rose up in him: an ambitious, certain fury. He would not allow his soul to be erased. Not like this.

'But you are wrong!' Tristan shouted. 'Your reasoning is incorrect. They will see that.'

He advanced on the rector, his fists trembling at his sides, the adrenaline surging again. The rector's stance was as steady as his stare. He didn't yield a centimetre.

'I know what you are going to say.'

'Are you mocking me?' Tristan had screamed in rage before.

Still the rector was unmoved. 'You think I cheated.'

'Of course you cheated. You had been watching me, through the walls of my room. You observed my meditation. You blocked my method by introducing her, by making it impossible for me to take my mind from the game.'

'That is true,' the rector said.

'Then you proved nothing!' Tristan felt the triumph as his argument grew solid. 'All you have shown is that under the right circumstances I can be anticipated, but put anyone under enough pressure and they become predictable. Set light to their house and they will flee it. That's all that happened here. It establishes nothing more than how badly I wanted to see her!'

'So you are claiming that under other circumstances you might have foiled me?'

The rector's calm caused Tristan to hesitate. He felt his certainty leaking from him, leaving his anger to tremble unsupported.

'Yes.'

'And how would you have done that?'

Tristan's mouth opened but the words were blocked by understanding. The truth appeared with sudden clarity and his legs grew unsteady beneath him.

'It is all right, Tristan.'

'It is not. You have taken it all.'

'It was never there to take.'

The rector put his hand on Tristan's shoulder. He eased his shaking body to the ground. 'Kneel with me, Tristan.'

'And do what, pray?'

'Yes, we shall pray for God's grace.' There was no irony in the rector's voice. They faced the completed puzzle together, the symbol of the greatest martyr, stolen by the Christians for their own macabre ends. They had knelt side-by-side like this once before, at the time of his father's death. This time Tristan felt his loss might take him under.

The rector spoke gently, as if reciting a prayer. 'Free will is an illusion, Tristan. You see that now. It is an illusion because the very concept is contradictory. You might have been able to find within yourself a kind of randomness that I could have not anticipated. I am not sure, but I admired your efforts and I cheated to block you. But that is what freedom must look like. It must be random, it must float free of every cause.

'I was younger than you when I first encountered this. I was walking towards a beggar with a coin in my pocket, and I knew I faced a moral choice. He was only a child and looked up at me, pleading. I stopped and thought, *God is watching me, and He wants me to do what is right.* So I looked within myself, hoping to discover His will.

'But you know what I found? What we all find when we try to pick apart our decisions. A collection of desires, expectations and prejudices. The jumble from which we construct every choice. I had been told by my parents never to give to beggars, that it only encouraged them and made their problems worse. I had heard a priest say the same thing. I had earned that coin, and knew just how I wished to spend it. And yet, against this were those eyes, the hunger in the way he held his body, the great feeling of empathy welling up in me. All these things mattered. They all needed to be considered.

'But then what happens? How do we move from influence to decision? We all know how it feels. It is as if some other self, some soul, weighs up these factors and then chooses the best path. But this is incoherent. Either we weigh the factors by instinct—a kind of algorithm, which is what I used to predict your actions—or we do what you tried to do, and open ourselves to randomness. We can have freedom, or we can have will, but it makes no sense to speak of having both.'

It was true. And now that Tristan understood, he found it impossible to believe it hadn't always been obvious.

'What did you do?' Tristan asked. 'With the beggar.'

The rector smiled.

'I could not decide so I let the coin decide for me. I flipped it in the air. Heads he would have it; tails it was mine.'

'And which was it?'

'Neither. He snatched it from the air before it hit the ground and ran off with his prize.'

They sat in silence, Tristan as much a part of the room as the walls that surrounded him, nailed to his future, unable to wriggle, or even protest.

'So why the test?' Tristan asked. 'Why not just explain this?'

'An argument has no force when it runs against our deepest intuitions. The council might have understood the argument, but they would not have believed it. They needed to see the demonstration. Just like you did.'

'How can you do this? How can you take it all from us?'

'I have taken nothing.'

'You have taken our belief,' Tristan said. 'What are we without it? We are nothing.'

'You are wrong,' the rector replied. 'There is still God's grace. And remember, if none of us is responsible, then none of us is past forgiveness. Augustine understood this, even though he resisted it.'

Tristan's head began to spin and his stomach gave a threatening lurch. Perhaps it was the shock of the game's violence. It was possible that he had taken a blow to the head. Or the greater shock of realising that whatever he did now, he could no longer claim to be the architect of his future.

'You need to stand now, Tristan. There is very little time.'

'To do what?' Tristan allowed himself to be pulled to his feet. The spinning turned to a wobble and the cross before him split into two and then four.

'To get you to the girl, and then both of you out of the City.'

'Why would we leave the City?'

'The Holy Council will not accept defeat easily. It will want you to confess that you were working to a script.'

'But I wasn't,' Tristan said.

'No, and you will not lie easily. I don't wish to be responsible for your torture.'

'Where will we go?'

'To the heathen settlements.' The rector handed him an envelope. 'There are papers in here, and instructions on how to find the people who will help you.'

Tristan said nothing. He stood gormless before his teacher.

'Quickly,' the rector said.

'If they come for me, won't they also come for you?'

'I would never have come this far without powerful friends, Tristan. The council knows that.'

But there was fear in the rector's voice; he could not hide it.

'Hurry,' he urged again. 'I am offering you freedom.'

'No,' Tristan replied as the truth bubbled to the surface. 'There is no freedom, remember.'

'Be slow to judge that,' the rector warned. 'The question is more subtle than you can imagine. God's grace goes with you, Tristan. Wear your fate well. It is what He asks of us.'

Again he offered his hand, and this time Tristan gripped it tight, tears blurring his vision further.

'Thank you,' he replied, although he couldn't say why he felt gratitude.

It was two years since Tristan had breathed the outside air and its sharpness threatened to overwhelm him. He stumbled on a raised paving stone and Simon caught him at the elbow.

'Careful, we must not draw attention to ourselves.'

The City was caught in the gloaming. Tristan felt the colour fading from his body as the aches of combat took hold. He was led to the workers' quarter, where he had not walked since childhood. His past presented itself as a stranger. Tristan had grown used to the meagre comforts of St Augustine's, and here the iron roofs and ill-fitting walls seemed built to the scale of children. The smell of the streets rose up in Tristan's nostrils, the stench of hopelessness. Simon stopped and pointed to a window yellowed by the dim glow of a single candle.

'That is it,' he said. 'That is her room. The rest is up to you. Go well.'

Tristan turned to the small window, his every thought suspended. No new impulse could rise without her; until they spoke, all was swirling, breathless possibility. He edged towards the glow, keeping in the shadows. He wasn't ready to be seen.

Grace sat at the edge of the bed, her head tilted as she brushed her hair. Tristan breathed in at the sight of her, cursing his memory for its inadequacy. Her face was more perfect than he had dared imagine. The candle danced, and he watched shadows lick her eyes, her lips, her nose. He was thrilled by her closeness. He whispered the name he had never spoken. *Grace.*

Tristan willed her to stay where she was—he could have watched her all night; but she knew nothing of his yearnings and stood to stretch her hands high above her head. She approached a small table by the window. Tristan could hear the gentle splashing of water. He followed her long fingers as she washed her face. She looked up, peering out into his darkness as if she had noticed him. This was the moment. *Call out to her,* Tristan's mind commanded. *Move into the light.* But his stubborn legs didn't move and his feckless lips stayed silent.

Tristan heard a knock within, small and muffled. Grace turned to face the door, her body straight and proud. A tall man, cast in shadow, walked towards her, stopping just before the point of touching. It was only then that the light of the candle fell on him and Tristan could see that he was naked. The man nodded his instruction. Tristan stood helpless as Grace pulled her gown slowly over her head, the muscles of her back knotted in the shallow light. Unclothed she knelt before the man. He turned to the candle and with his wicked breath extinguished the light.

Tristan backed away, numb and exhausted. He fell to his knees and splashed vomit on the muddy ground. His stomach, his past, his self: all returned to the dirt.

§

'And that is how it happened. That is the story of how I lost my place in the world.'

'I did see you,' she whispered. 'I saw you there.'

Tristan felt something sharp and hard in his mouth and worked it to the front with his swollen tongue. A broken tooth. He spat it clear and waited for her to speak. She owed him nothing, no explanation or apology, but still he hoped.

'I'm sorry.' Her fingers squeezed his forearm.

'No, I am sorry,' he said. 'Mine is the greater crime.'

'You haven't heard my story,' she reminded him.

'No, but I know how mine ends.'

'I think you need me to forgive you,' Grace said.

'For what?'

'Whatever it is you think you have done.'

'What I have done,' Tristan said, 'is unforgivable.'

'There's no such thing.'

'You will change your mind.'

'My mind doesn't change easily,' she replied.

Just when Tristan thought there were no new depths to plumb, it hit him: a surge of pain so utterly compelling he lost all concept of time. There was only now, this exploding moment of torture. He did not scream; even sound could not escape its pull.

When it left, it took his last scraps of energy. Exhaustion insisted itself upon him and he felt himself tumbling into unconsciousness.

'Tristan. Tristan!'

Grace had been speaking but he had not heard her. Now she pulled at his broken shoulder. He felt his body sway with the movement, but it was not his body. He was outside it now, an observer.

'You can't fall asleep.'

'I am tired,' he mumbled.

'We are both tired,' she said.

'No.' Tristan shook his head. 'I can't do this any more. It is over.'

'Not yet.' She would not allow it. 'We will outlast the darkness.'

'You don't know that.' Tristan could feel himself shrinking from the world.

'Sit up. Come on, move.'

Somehow she had an arm beneath him and was urging him forward. His stomach tightened and he began to cough, desperate choking claims on the air, folding one into the other. There was, it seemed, no denying her. He was awake again.

'I will tell you how I came to leave the convent,' she said. 'But listen well. I will take it personally if you fall asleep.'

Grace's Story

The City had little trouble providing death and there were never more than a few days between passings. Grace slipped out once a week, twice if there was a need. The job she had given herself was plain, but it wasn't simple: she sought to offer comfort where no comfort was available. It was her instinctive response to the weight of death on the mourners' shoulders, the salt of tears on their cheeks. And to the warmth that came from performing a humble task well. She found strength in routine and dedication and believed her work brought her closer to God, as she had been taught in the convent. She never lost her faith, even if it was necessary to reinvent Him each day.

It came as no surprise that one evening an angel should emerge from the shadows at the side of the chapel. 'What are you?' she asked, but he gave no answer. Still, it was enough that he had shown himself. She knew then that her work was finding favour.

The first times Grace escaped the convent were terrifying. Every sound or shift in the pressure of the air convinced her she was being watched. She developed an ache in her neck from being permanently tense, waiting for a bony hand to reach out of the darkness. But it never did. Not on the first night, or the second, or even the tenth. Grace began to relax. Seeing the angel convinced her she was being protected and she began to take more risks, leaving earlier in the night, taking the shorter route through wider, better-lit streets.

And then it was over.

The entrance to the passage was well concealed and Grace always paused to test the silence before she stepped back inside the convent. But Sister Monica made no sound. She was kneeling before the altar, her eyes wide against the gloom. Grace heard a great roaring in her ears, the sound of her future being sucked out of existence. Instinctively she fell to her knees, ready to play the innocent fool, frightened and remorseful.

'Sister,' she whispered, 'I have been weak and thoughtless, but I am sorry for my sin. It was just this once and I am glad that you have found me for it has saved me from further temptation…'

Sister Monica laughed in her face. 'You are a wicked child, Grace. You always have been. I am surprised you lasted this long.'

There were no rituals for expulsion. The nuns didn't want to make heroes of the departed. They didn't even bother with a final whipping. Grace was stripped of her robes, dressed in a coarse hessian smock and escorted out the front gate. The bolt was slid shut behind her and she was left standing before the City, a stranger fallen to earth without connections or prospects, her future of no interest to those who passed. In the cold dawn light Grace knew that a wrong move could kill her, yet she had no idea what a right move might be. She had felt fear many times, but it had never before held her with such certainty.

The grey sky was lightening in the east and Grace felt the chill of the departing night shiver through her. She began to walk, hoping movement might be enough to keep hopelessness at bay. She chose her path at random, her mind paralysed by shock. It happens this quickly, she realised, the rubbing out of a life.

By nightfall Grace was hungry and aching and no closer to knowing how she might survive. She headed for St Paul's Chapel because she couldn't think where else to go. There were no passings scheduled that night and she found the doors locked. She made herself as comfortable as she could in the alley where she had seen the angel, dimly hoping that if he intended to save her this was where she could be easily found. The cold bit into her bones. Fifteen years old, and fading. If Mary had not found her, she would have died there.

Mary was a young mother Grace had comforted at a passing some months before. Grace didn't recognise her— grief has a way of melting one face into another—but Mary remembered Grace. Later she would explain that bereaved mothers often walked past the chapel even though it was strictly forbidden. It was the only place they had to mourn, and to renegotiate their deals with God.

Mary insisted Grace come back to her home. Grace tried to resist; the City looked unkindly on those who harboured troublemakers and Grace had no desire to put Mary at risk. Mary would not be moved. When she had needed it most, Grace had been there to offer comfort, she explained, and now it filled her with gladness to be able to return the favour.

It was clear from her small dwelling that Mary could not afford to play the hostess. What's more, Mary's husband, Anthony, was a tiler and depended on the Holy Council for his contracts. If people chose to make trouble it could cost him his livelihood. He should have turned Grace away—all three of them knew it—but his heart was weak with kindness and he raised no objections. He smiled and he returned to his evening task of weaving straw insulation in preparation for the winter. Grace was given food and shelter without any talk of recompense. For two long months she didn't leave the tiny building, for fear of bringing Mary and Anthony further trouble.

When Mary fell pregnant again Grace knew the time to leave had come. No matter what goodness Mary possessed, her child had first claim to it. And Mary had suffered two passings; she needed every scrap of food Anthony could provide for her. Each morning Grace woke determined this would be the day she would go. She would make it easy for them, slipping out into the darkness before they could object. But at nightfall all three of them were still together, each finding excuses to forgo their share of the inadequate meal.

Fear had Grace pinned there. No matter how much it hurt her to impose on them, she knew the cold City would kill her within a week. The spirit was willing, but the flesh refused to die. It was almost a relief when Mary finally raised the issue.

The winter had grown vindictive and Grace sat in front of the fire with a blanket wrapped around her. Mary had been at the markets and said nothing as she settled next to her guest. She took Grace's hands in her own and Grace, feeling the iciness, assumed she was trying to warm them. Then she saw Mary had been crying.

'It's all right,' Grace said. 'I know you can't afford to keep me now. I wouldn't want you to try. You must think of the baby. I am sorry I let it come to this. I will be gone before Anthony is home.'

Mary shook her head; the sadness in her eyes was magnified by tears.

'No, Grace. You would die.'

'Then that is what will happen,' Grace replied.

'You will stay here, Grace.' Mary spoke quietly, with the same voice the nuns taught the girls to use when ministering to the sick and dying. 'But we can no longer keep you. You need to bring money into the home.'

'I would do anything, of course, but no one would employ me.'

Mary knew as well as Grace did how the City worked. Graduates of the convents took jobs as servants. Those from better homes trained as teachers and nurses, to pass the time before they met their husbands. That was all there was. No expelled girl could hope to find employment in the City. Grace looked to Mary, hoping desperately there was more to the world than she could imagine. It was not impossible. The convent had raised the concealment of truth to an art form.

Mary squeezed Grace's hand and stared at the muted flames.

'There are men, Grace, who would pay to lie with you.'

At first Grace didn't understand. She looked for a clue, but Mary's eyes were fixed on the ground. 'I would not ask this of you if it…'

'I will do it,' Grace assured her, understanding little of what it was she promised. Whatever it was, it had to be better than dying. 'I owe it to you. I do not mind.'

The next day, when Anthony was out at work, Mary explained the rudimentaries of sex and contraception. It was difficult for them both but Mary was thinking of her child and Grace of her life; they understood there are worse things to bear than embarrassment. But there was still one thing that Grace did not understand. How would they manage the risk of strangers entering the home? The front door was the house's only entrance and curtains in the workers' quarter twitched at the smallest sound. Mary's answer surprised her.

'There are rules for us, Grace, and rules for them. Most of them do not care what the people round here see. Why should they? This is another country to them.'

Mary was right. In the months that followed Grace had sex with traders and judges, with lawyers and bankers, bishops and architects, and not one of them was concerned by the gossip of the slums. Only one man came to her in secret, a priest who visited every second Friday. He called in the hours of daylight so that everyone could see he carried the paraphernalia of the confessional. In fact he insisted on hearing Grace's confession at the end of his exertions, and Mary's too, and even that stopped seeming strange eventually.

At first Grace was terrified. She knew so little and felt powerless because of it. In time though she discovered her ignorance only served to increase her worth, and as the weeks collected into months habit dulled her fear. She came to see the men for what they were: tourists to a land whose language they barely spoke, each in his own way more frightened than she was.

§

'It's hard to explain it, Tristan, and you won't want to hear it, but sometimes a closeness developed. Some days I felt the thing we shared was our terror.'

'Don't say it,' Tristan demanded. 'Do not make them worthy of your pity.'

'I left my shame at the passings, Tristan. You should have done the same.'

'They hated you.'

'Some of them did,' she agreed. 'For some of them hatred was all they had left. There was one who wept when he was finished, and had me hold him as a mother holds a child. One told me jokes and made me laugh, and there was one who paid just to look at me—'

'I don't want to hear it!' Tristan heard himself shouting.

'Then you're a hypocrite.'

'You don't understand.'

'Perhaps not, but at least I'm prepared to learn.'

'I don't want to hear about them,' he said again. 'I don't want to hear about the men.'

'Can I tell you that they paid me well, and every last coin went to Mary?'

Tristan said nothing. He felt foolish to have spoken, but that didn't diminish his pain.

'I'm sorry. Go on.'

'Money changes everything, Tristan. At last I was contributing. For the first time since I lost Josephine, I felt it might be possible to be happy again. I was going to stay after the baby was born and help with the mothering. Mary was a good woman. I even imagined that one day the two of us might become friends.'

Later Grace would meet girls on the street who would tell her that their lives unravelled slowly and, by the time they realised, it was too late for repairs. Grace though could name the exact moment fate turned on her. It happened two weeks before Mary was due to give birth. Mary moved into the house of a friend. She had some money this time and was able to share the expenses of the larger warmer home, closer to the midwives. Grace stayed behind with Anthony. He was a quiet man and she saw him only at meal times. Grace knew he was more shy than aloof and appreciated the small efforts he made to make her smile as they sat and ate together.

Anthony was a good and loyal man. That was how Mary always described him, and Grace had seen nothing to suggest otherwise. He had risked his livelihood to take her in, and had never once made her feel unwelcome.

But that night he knocked on her door and stood before her naked. Grace met his eye, hoping shame might overcome him, but he didn't blink. His face was set with an expression she recognised well. The look of entitlement.

§

'I saw you standing out there that night, you know.'

'You didn't say anything.'

'I was waiting for you. I thought you had a message. And then, when he came in, I thought you were there to keep me safe, to give me strength.'

'That's a childish way of thinking.'

'I was a child. But I should have called out. It might have changed things.'

'Things can't be changed.'

'You're angry.'

It was true. How could he not be angry?

'Not with you.'

'Say you forgive me.'

'Forgiving you is not the problem,' Tristan told her. He listened to her silence, guessing at the thoughts that gathered there.

'I don't understand,' she said.

And he wasn't ready to explain. Not yet.

'Tell me more,' Tristan asked. 'Tell me how you escaped the City.'

§

Anthony stayed no longer than his need required. Grace walked to the window and peered out into the darkness. Her angel had gone. But she had seen him. That must have meant something. Perhaps he had come to warn her. Her mistake then was not reading him. She felt the window ledge hard against her ribs and pushed against it so that for a moment she might feel a new kind of pain. She would leave. That was it. The angel had wanted her to follow him and she had paid the price for hesitating.

Grace lay on her bed and felt the house close in around her. Once the creaking had comforted her; now it felt as if the walls meant to crush her as she slept. In the next room she heard Anthony moving through his bedtime rituals as if nothing had happened. She compiled a list of the things she would take with her. A short list: hers was not an accumulating life. She waited until she heard Anthony snoring, and then crept into the street.

She never knew how he explained her absence to his wife, or even if Mary survived the birth. They disappeared into the past, as Grace disappeared into the night. Only months before she would have walked to her death, but the City would have to work harder to take her now that she'd seen its leaders naked. And her angel was close. She wouldn't die on his watch.

St Mark's was a modest church, built in a hurry to serve the growing population of the workers' quarter. Grace sat patiently on its doorstep, Anthony's coat wrapped tight around her, and waited for the dawn. Father Peter arrived first. He stopped cold when he saw her, and Grace thought how the grey light made him look like a statue, though stone was rarely wasted on the craven.

'What are you doing here?' he whispered.

'You can speak normally, Father,' Grace replied. 'There is no one but God to hear us, and He already knows.'

She watched with satisfaction as her most timid customer shrank before her.

'But, you…mustn't.'

It was not difficult to imagine how Father Peter had washed up on the shores of such an unsplendid parish. He was an uninspiring figure, short and round with fearful eyes and a voice that struggled beneath its load.

'But you visited me, Father, regularly,' Grace said.

'No, go. Go back to your home.' He shooed at her with his hands as if she was a pigeon defecating on a holy bust, but Grace didn't flinch.

'I can't go back, Father,' she explained. 'I have been mistreated there. And now you must help me.'

'Why should I help you?' he said, but she saw in his eyes that he understood.

'Because you are a priest, Father, and it is what priests do.'

Grace offered a guileless smile. She stood and motioned to the church's locked door.

'Will you let me in?'

Father Peter was a fearful man but not a stupid one, and once the door was closed behind them his confidence returned. He told her that her suggestion of staying on as his housekeeper was impossible. All such appointments needed approval from the Holy Council.

'Well, I can't live on the streets, Father,' Grace replied, clenching her toes to control the shaking in her legs. She knew her life depended on this, the hiding of her desperation. 'I am staying here until you can think of a way to help.'

Time slowed and Grace's fear stretched with it. Father Peter looked at her, his own terror rippling the air between them. Grace waited. If he speaks first, she told herself, I have won. She had to believe in something. She watched the priest's pale skin turn blue as the rising sun pierced a stained-glass window.

'Wait here,' he told her. 'Don't move. I will be back within the hour.'

'Why should I trust you?' Grace asked, not daring to smile.

'Because you have no choice,' Father Peter answered.

Good to his word the priest returned before the sun had warmed the waking air. He handed Grace an envelope.

'What is it?'

'Your pass out of the City,' he told her. 'Present these papers at the Great Gate tonight and you will be allowed to leave.'

'And go where?'

'There is a depot outside the walls where the trucks have their kilometres checked. Go there and ask for James.'

'And what will James do for me?'

'He will take you to the heathen settlements.'

She didn't like the easy way the details came to him, as if this was not the first time he had made such arrangements.

'How am I to support myself when I get there?' Grace demanded, angry he could dispose of her with so little trouble.

'By doing what you do best.' Father Peter smiled. His confidence was back now that he'd managed to wipe her from his shoe. 'James will take you to the place.'

Grace slapped him hard, hearing the contact ring out through the church, but the satisfaction barely outlasted the impression of her fingers on his cowardly face.

James had black hair, greased close to his ratty skull, and eyes that wandered freely from the bumping road to Grace's shaking body. He was carrying a shipment of bibles for sale in the heathen settlements.

'Holy books and whores,' he said, 'our only exports.' The observation took him to the point of choking, and Grace felt the fine spray of his amusement settle on her leg.

She looked back only once at the great walls of the City growing smaller in the distance; the past telescoped out of view and the future became a hazy smudge of light on the horizon.

After the cool regulated world of the City, the settlement seemed to Grace to be a land dissolved in chaos: a million jostling souls, strange unreadable patterns of need emerging from the clamour of light and colour and want. James stopped the truck outside a beautiful white-painted house that stood between two huge towers of glass and steel. He led her to the front door and knocked. She felt neither fear nor gratitude. For now, it was enough to be alive.

'What's in there?' Grace asked.

'Your future,' James answered. 'Good luck. Who knows, if they like you I might even see you again some day.'

He winked and let his gaze slide down to her breasts.

'Hello, Martha, a convent girl fresh from the City.'

'Can you vouch for her?'

'She comes highly recommended.'

Martha, the madam of the house, had applied her make-up in the way a plasterer applies render, but still the cracks were visible. Her hair, cut short and close to her head, was dyed an improbable red. Her dress, black and of the finest fabric Grace had ever seen, swayed loosely about her delicate frame and a huge ring of gold dangled from each ear, as if to keep her from floating free. Once she had been beautiful, and the memory of beauty lingered in her eyes. Her expression was warm but careful, appraising, and her voice was startling.

'What is your name?'

'Grace, Ma'am.'

'A convent girl?'

Grace nodded.

'Have you been whipped?'

The room was warm and the furniture more opulent

than Grace had ever seen. She considered lying but there was no hiding the scars.

'Yes, but many years ago.'

'Let's see, then. Lift that dress off and turn around.'

Grace did as she was told and felt the pressure of bony fingers running along the hard raised skin.

'You're lucky: they healed badly. It's a nice rough contour. We'll take you. Turn around. Look at me. We'll test you and if you're clean there's a room for you with the other girls. Staying clean is your responsibility. We'll pay you well if the clients like you. I'm sure they will. That's a great blemish and you seem shy, which is what they look for. You're lucky. I'll keep you safe.'

The woman pulled her close. Grace was as numb as the scars on her back.

There were twelve girls altogether and they slept off the premises in a hostel that was clean and comfortable. The girls were friendly and at the same time wary, an attitude Grace remembered well from her convent days. She tried to be careful too, yet in those first few weeks she laughed more than she had in all the years before. And for the first time in her life she received a wage. The money felt strange in her hand, like the first tickling of a new disease. When she wasn't working she was free to explore, but the rush of the streets overwhelmed her and she preferred to lie on her bed reading the tattered books and magazines she found on a shelf next to the linen.

Settlement men were different of course—their clothes and their way of talking—but none was unfamiliar. It was the same mix of the shy and the confident, the polite and the demanding, the frightened and the frightening. Until Grace met Pete, the men held no surprises.

Initially she mistook him for a first-timer. He hung in the doorway as if waiting to be invited in and was careful to keep his eyes from her body. When he walked his movements were gentle. His narrow shoulders and small hands suggested a life free from labour, and when she led him to the edge of the bed he remained standing, like an unannounced visitor not wanting to impose.

'What would you like?' Grace asked. Although his light hair was thinning she saw he had the eyes of a child, ready to tip into tears or laughter.

'It's a little unusual.' He dipped his eyes and a blush worried its way across his cheeks.

'You will do well to surprise me,' Grace said.

'My name is Pete. I would like you to like me.'

'I already like you,' Grace replied. It was a game and she was good at it, finding the right words to relax them.

'No, genuinely like me.'

'I'm not sure what you mean.'

He sat down and let her take his hand.

'I've never been here before. I suppose that's obvious. Or maybe all your clients pretend that. I don't know. I don't want to tell you about myself, not too much. But I am sad. I haven't always been sad, but life, it catches us unawares. It shouldn't, but it does. And I need to be able to tell somebody I am sad. This, well, it's honest, isn't it? That's what I decided.

There's no pretending. I'm paying you to do as I please. And as I please is for you to listen to me and talk to me, and if I am lucky you will like me. And if you don't, I don't want you to pretend. Is that all right?'

Grace nodded. He was right: it wasn't unusual for men to start this way. But Pete spoke in a way that made her want to believe him.

'And when I like you?'

'Then I suppose I'd like to fuck you,' he admitted with a smile. 'But not today. Today I would like to talk to you.'

This too she had heard before. Perhaps he even believed it. But no man was to leave unrelieved. On this point the madam was most insistent.

'The frightened ones need you to lead them,' she explained. 'They would never have come here if they didn't want you, and they'll never be back again if you don't give them a reason to return.'

'I chose this place because it has convent girls,' Pete continued. 'And I am interested in that. I am interested in talking about God.'

That part, she had to admit, was new. He used his hour and then paid for a second, and all the time they did nothing but talk about God. He questioned her about her education and her beliefs, and Grace did what she always did: wove truth and tale together, keeping close to herself those things that mattered most—Josephine and the angel.

Grace was worried when Pete left with no more than a handshake, and she expected to be punished for it. But he was back three nights later, and in the months that followed

Grace saw him on average twice a week. He told her he taught psychology at one of the universities, and she believed him. He knew more than anybody she had ever met and was a kind and patient teacher. Soon her thoughts were patterned with his fingerprints and with every new thing he told her she yearned to learn more. He brought her books to read; histories were her favourite. One morning he took her out in his car to show her the places he had talked about: the street where he grew up, the school of his childhood, the restaurant where he worked washing dishes through his student years.

Grace had little trouble convincing Pete she liked him. The learning, the laughing, the sex—all of it made her feel important. She found herself wishing the girls from the convent could see what she had become. Some nights thoughts of Pete kept her from sleeping. For the first time since the death of Josephine, Grace had a friend. When she asked him if he was her angel he laughed and ran his finger down her scars. When he brought her gifts and told her she had saved him, she cried.

And then one week he didn't visit. One week turned to two, then three. His absence clawed at her and the only thing she could think of doing was the thing she knew she mustn't do.

§

'Why were you surprised? You were just a whore to him.' It was easy for Tristan to hate the man she described. The affection in her voice tore at him like broken steel.

'And what am I to you?' she demanded, her voice rising to his challenge.

'You went to him, didn't you?'

'They told me if I ever initiated contact with a client I would be gone,' Grace said. 'But he didn't feel like a client. I thought...'

She finished with a whimper, whether in pain or sadness Tristan couldn't know. Either way it softened him.

'I am sorry,' he said.

'Thank you.'

'What happened?'

'Nothing surprising. He had shown me where his university was. I found his office. He was there with a student. I suppose she was my age, a year or two older perhaps. They were laughing together when I walked in. He let go of her and stood to face me. Neither of us spoke. There wasn't any need. He must have phoned them. My bag had been packed by the time I got back.'

'What did you do?'

'I found the cheapest room I could. I lived off the food others discarded. When my money ran out I learned to work the streets.'

There was a toughness to her voice. It had been there all night but it was only now that it made sense to him. If this was a competition she would outlast him. But then, just as he thought he understood, her voice turned tender.

'We had our stories, we street girls. We could all recite the circumstances of our imagined salvation. There wasn't one of us who wasn't infected with a fantasy. Mine was of an angel. He'd appear again, I told them on the evenings we could find cheap drink. And he'd take me away from it all.

'You were my story, you see. I didn't believe it, except when I was telling it. That was our rule, I suppose: you had to believe, just for as long as you were telling the story.' Grace laughed, a warm sound speckled with irony. 'One day you would appear again, and this time I wouldn't let you leave. I would grab you by the arm and cling to you, and that would be the end of my suffering.

'And you did appear. You drove up in this car…I cannot tell you how strange it was to see you. I didn't believe it at first. I couldn't believe it. You found me, Tristan. No matter what comes of us, I am glad of that. I am glad you found me.'

'You mustn't be,' Tristan replied.

Never in his life had he been more certain.

PART 3

First Light

Tristan watched the outline of Grace's head, failing to make the connection.

Grace noticed first.

'It's getting lighter.'

'The rain's stopped,' he replied. 'Perhaps it is just the clouds clearing.'

'No, it's almost morning.' She spoke like a child awake too early on her birthday, willing light into the sky. 'We're going to be all right.'

Her optimism broke like a wave, threatening to capsize him. He wouldn't allow it. Not yet. She stared back at him, each looking into the darkness of the other's face, waiting to see.

Tristan squinted. He could make out only a hint of her face. Her eyes, which shone so bright in his memory, were shadowed pools, sunk deep in fear. They darted, searching as his did for the mirrored details of their decline. There was no colour yet; dried blood matted hair to her forehead in thick black lines. She tried to smile, revealing gaps where teeth had been.

He could find no word to describe the wreckage, no place in his mind into which this image could be slotted. It floated free, rising up even when he screwed his eyes tight against it.

'What is it?' she asked.

'I did this to you,' he said, counting his teeth with his swollen tongue. 'I did this.'

'We'll get out of here,' she replied. 'Soon, when it is properly light, the traffic will see us. Somebody will come.'

'Don't lie to me.'

'Don't think about it. Finish your story.'

'I've nothing left to tell,' Tristan lied, turning away, daring her to break the silence.

Grace took his hand. The fight was leaking out of her. It was over to others now. The car would be seen or it would not. Thus all things reduce.

Tristan looked again at Grace's hair, trying to make out something of its colour. There was nothing but shade. He closed his left eye, which throbbed the least of the two, and the world went dark again.

'What is it?'

'I can't see.'

'You have your eyes closed.'

'Only one of them.'

Tristan opened it to see Grace looking away.

'What is it?' He felt fear fall out in a rush. 'What can you see?'

'We are both hurt,' she mumbled, fixing her gaze on the shattered screen. 'It is to be expected.'

'Tell me what you see.'

'There is nothing to tell. Some swelling, that is all. A cut across your forehead. It doesn't look too bad.'

'You're lying.'

'Why would I lie?'

'To make it better.'

'We are not children.'

Tristan wriggled frantically, ignoring the fireworks of pain in his hip.

'What are you doing?'

'I want to see. I want to get to the mirror. I want to see.'

'And how will that help?'

'Then I'll know.'

'You won't know anything.'

In his panic Tristan couldn't find his reflection. He reached for Grace's neck.

'Tell me!' he screeched, feeling his fingers gain purchase in the yielding flesh. She didn't resist. Her face set in stony absence, a look he had seen on the monks when they meditated. He let go.

'I am sorry.'

'Again.'

'Yes, again.'

She waited before speaking, asserting the terms.

'I am no doctor, Tristan, but from what I can see, your eye is swollen almost closed.'

'What can you tell from that part that is open?'

'It is red.'

'Bloodshot?'

'More red than that. There is only red.'

Tristan raised his hand to his face. The movement was slow and clumsy. His fingers were too damaged to tell him much, and the rawness of his pulpy face sent him into retreat.

'You'll be all right,' she said.

'You say that more often than I say sorry.'

He could make out the window now, a white cobweb of fractures, yet resolute. The world beyond was taking distorted shape: the dark edge of a rock face, tall grass running to seed, and, beyond, the grey-blue of distance as the world dropped away. They had not hit the bottom. What was above them would determine the outcome. If they had settled beneath an overhang there was no way of their being seen from the road. Fate, determined yet unknowable.

'You should have called out,' Grace said. 'When you stood at my window, you should have called out.'

'What difference would it have made?' he said.

'We can never know.'

'No.'

'What happened to you that night?' she asked. 'How did you find me again?'

'What does it matter? They will find us or they won't. That is our story now.'

'I am interested.'

'You will wish you hadn't been.'

'Life is full of risks,' Grace replied.

'It is no risk. It is certain.'

'Then I will be responsible for my pain. I have told you how I came to be standing on the street. Now you must tell me how you came to be driving by.'

There was no avoiding her question. If they were to die, she deserved to know why. And if they were to live, she deserved the opportunity to hate him. His every instinct cried at him to lie to her, to lose the story in a tangle of invention, but he would not. Could not.

Tristan and Grace's Story

Tristan lifted his face from the dirt and snorted his nose free of vomit. Her window remained completely dark, but the memory of what he had seen could not be extinguished. He stood, but the world around him refused to settle. He swayed, uncertain. Wear your fate well, the rector had said, but that made no sense. Who was to say it was not his fate to fall back to the ground and die? How should such a defeat be worn? He lurched forward, his legs somehow aware of the need to move. He stumbled on. Not towards a future, but away from her. Away from the pain.

He found a low bridge and crept beneath it. He fell asleep as the sun rose, to the sounds of the occasional delivery truck rumbling overhead and a solitary bird singing to the daylight. When he woke again the sky had dimmed and his head throbbed from thirst and discomfort. Self-pity hung about him, but he needed to drink and that meant moving. He pissed into the dirty river then scrambled back to the road. He stood there waiting for some plan to take hold of him, listening for the familiar murmur of forming thoughts. His head though was quiet, as if his soul had returned to the hiding place. He looked over the side of the bridge and watched a discarded can float slowly past, tied to the black water's ooze.

He remembered the envelope the rector had given him and opened it. There were papers and money as well as an address. He knew the street; it ran close to the docks and old warehouses still remaining from the days commerce ran the river.

The address led him to a building that had once served as the headquarters of a grain merchant and, according to its tarnished plaque, had stood for more than a century as a memorial to hungry endeavour. Now it was reduced to a warren of bricks, a maze in which every turn took the visitor a little further from the reach of God. Tristan presented his papers and explained that he needed to leave the City. A man with thick lips and unruly eyebrows checked the money and shook his head.

'It's barely enough.'

It was a bad lie smoothed by habit, but Tristan had no energy for arguing. He was taken to a holding room until the next night fell and then smuggled past the gates in the back of a truck that bumped and rattled its way across the empty land.

Tristan would never forget the moment he arrived in

the heathen settlements. He stood where the truck had left him, fractured and uncomprehending. He had never seen so many people. The landscape wriggled with life like a leg of meat infested with maggots. It seemed that light and noise spilled through every crack. Tristan had been raised in a world where electricity was rationed and yet here, less than two hours of rutted track away, it was as if they struggled with a mighty surplus that had to be unloaded hot and buzzing into the streets before the whole place exploded.

The smugglers had provided Tristan with clothes. They were tatty but didn't mark him as an outsider. It felt unnatural to have shoes on his feet and he scuffed along the footpaths with the slack-jawed wonderment of a junkie. Great towers stretched up into the sky and soon his neck ached from looking up at them. He stopped at a shopfront window and looked at a display of television screens, each reduced to the fuzzing of the late-night disconnection. The unpatterned static provided a comfort of sorts and he stood numb before it.

Soon he realised he was not alone. Another man at the far end of the shopfront watched the same spectacle. For five empty minutes neither of them spoke. The other man's clothes and skin were filthy. But then he smiled, and Tristan almost cried with gratitude.

'That there's the big bang,' the stranger said, ambling forward and nodding at the screens. 'The static. It's the background radiation from the beginning of time itself. Now it's everywhere, a broken signal that can never be put back together. Beautiful, isn't it.'

'I too have broken apart,' Tristan said. It was all he had, his leaky truth.

'It happens to us all, brother,' the man replied. 'My name is William. Do you have a place to sleep tonight?'

Tristan shook his head, neither hopeful nor wary. He simply was. Life would happen to him now and he would let it, at least until the point where the sadness overwhelmed him.

'Then neither do I,' William chuckled. 'Do you have any drink on you?'

Again Tristan shook his head.

'Ah, well, there's a bigger problem. My name is William.'

'You already told me that.'

This news seemed to trouble the man.

'Have we met before?'

'No.'

'Well then, I don't see how I could have told you.' He eyed Tristan suspiciously.

'My mistake.'

William had once been a tall man. If he straightened to look the world in the eye he could be tall again. But he stooped further as he moved away, his feet planted wide as if each moved in opposition to the other. He turned back to Tristan.

'Are you coming or aren't you?'

Tristan shrugged and followed, and so his first night in the heathen settlements did not kill him.

§

'I lived long enough to find you. For that we can blame William, or the big bang, or any point in between.'

She said nothing. He couldn't tell if she was still listening and perhaps it no longer mattered. He was rolling now, tumbling down the slope of their final chapter.

§

William led Tristan to the basement of a car park where a group of homeless people had staked their claim. A fire burned in a drum and twenty or so figures circled in a dance of attraction and repulsion, drawn to the warmth yet wary of one another, each as uncertain as an electron, as sensitive to observation.

Planted on the only piece of furniture Tristan could see, a once-stately couch now grown humble, was a woman so fat she may well have been stranded. Two boys some years younger than Tristan sat one on either side of her swollen ankles, their jealous eyes on the pile of junk that served as fuel for the fire. The massive woman softly patted their heads and Tristan was sure he heard purring.

'Fat Annie,' William whispered as they approached. Tristan did not know if he was sharing a joke or explaining her proper title.

'This is Tristan,' William announced, as if presenting his queen with a captured prize from a distant land. She looked Tristan up and down. He felt nothing but weariness and a thick fuzzy sense of disconnection, as if he was descending into a dream.

'What brings you here?' asked the queen. Her voice was melodic, a throatful of notes resonating in her enormous bosom. Her eyes shone bright within fleshy caves.

'My life,' Tristan answered, not trying to amuse her but nonetheless bringing forth a laugh that gurgled its way up the scale.

'Then you have stories to tell,' Fat Annie said. 'Come, sit beside me.'

That there was no space into which Tristan might settle seemed to cause Annie no concern. Tristan edged cautiously forward and she made a great show of shifting her bulk to the side, although this was ultimately as hopeless as pushing water from the shore. He sat and felt her great mass spill back over him.

'This is cosy,' she giggled. 'Tell me, where are you from?'

'The City of God,' Tristan answered. He saw no point in lying. He saw no point in anything. She grasped his knee in delight.

'I knew it.' Fat Annie raised her voice so the others could hear her. 'People, we have an angel amongst us. Come and listen to his stories.'

Seven or eight of them shuffled her way: curious, suspicious, perhaps resenting Tristan's place on the throne. Fat Annie produced a bottle of dark liquid and after swigging heavily offered it to Tristan. It burned his throat, his stomach and his head. He thought vaguely that she might be poisoning him; his head felt light and unpossessed. His story stuttered forth.

The street people were a credulous, encouraging

audience. They appeared fascinated by the strange otherness of life in the City and would not let him skimp on details. Tristan told them what he could of St Augustine's, the rector and the experiments, and they grunted and wheezed their understanding. As Tristan's story unfolded, a small hope rose in him. Perhaps these strangers would expose the rector's tricks and free him from his failure. But that wasn't where their interest lay. It was Tristan's despair they found comfort in and, as the night grew small and the bottle emptied, Tristan found something similar in theirs.

It was the oddest feeling: a procession of filthy strangers making sounds of comfort and tapping him on the back as they dispersed, their eyes deep with a sadness he didn't recognise. They were welcoming him, he realised.

Tristan sensed he was being ushered to his own funeral, but he offered no resistance. Someone gave him a dirty piece of cardboard to protect him from the concrete's piercing cold. He lay on it and was surprised to see Fat Annie lumbering his way. She said nothing as she eased herself down behind him and he offered no complaint; the night was cold and her huge body generated unusual warmth. He found himself curling up as if a child again, and when her strangulated snoring started he backed further against her. As the night dissolved him he remembered Madame Grey, the woman who long ago had filled the mother-sized hole in his boyish imagination. The thought of it undid him and he felt tears turn icy on his cheeks.

The next morning Tristan woke cold and sore. His bones

ached and his head was cut in two by a pain so sharp he could feel its edges. He looked at William, who was stooped over him, shaking him by the shoulder.

'Come on, there's work to be done.'

'What work?' Tristan asked.

'Work that keeps you from dying,' William said.

'I'm happy to die,' Tristan said, and it was no exaggeration. Giving in would have been as easy as closing his eyes. A great fleshy arm draped across him and he felt her breath rotten but gentle in his ear.

'Leave the poor boy alone.' Fat Annie pulled Tristan close and he felt himself disappearing into her warmth. 'You stay there if you need to. You can start tomorrow as easy as today.'

Great globs of sadness dislodged deep in Tristan's stomach and made their way to his throat. He pulled away from her, embarrassed, and wiped his eyes with his sleeve.

'I'm all right,' he answered in reply to the question that hadn't been asked. 'Show me what you need me to do.'

Over the following weeks William became Tristan's teacher. He showed him how scavenging, theft and begging could be woven into a living of sorts. Each night they gathered in the basement around the fire's puny warmth and offered Annie their pickings. Tristan did what he could, but he was poorly suited to the work and felt ashamed by the little he contributed. Fat Annie assessed the bounty and then shared it amongst them all.

'Why not each of us keep what we find?' Tristan asked William. It pained him that others might think he was a burden.

'Because keeping what you find is how it's done in the settlements,' William replied, 'and it's the settlements' way of doing things that's put us here.'

'But it's unfair.'

'There are kinds of unfair,' William said. 'And this is the good kind.'

Each night, as darkness tightened around them, they were drawn back to Annie's generous laugh and encouraged to tell stories. Tristan became known as the saint. On evenings when drink made them sentimental, they had him lead them in prayer. A more pious, solemn congregation a pastor couldn't hope for. It wasn't unusual for the men to cry over verses long polished of meaning. Although the sadness didn't leave him—it was always there humming in the background, threatening to bloom into hopelessness—the life became familiar and in its routine Tristan found a sort of comfort. The weeks turned to months and piece by piece he lost hold of the memory of self. He was one of them now, tangled and adrift on the same tide. Until winter came.

Storms swept in and there was no escaping the cold. The number in the basement swelled, making the sharing of their spoils more difficult. Suspicion and jealousy diminished them. Sleep became a luxury, stolen, like everything else, in small inadequate packages. But with sleep came nightmares. Every night Tristan was woken by screaming. Often it was his own. He stayed away from the drink—he had little stomach for it—but there was no escaping its corrosive power. Frightened men turned angry without warning; watchfulness became the natural state. The community lived on a knife's edge, or if not a knife then a broken bottle or a length of discarded iron. An imagined wrong, a septic grudge: the violence was never far away. Despite the stories they shared, Tristan lay each night with strangers, each slowly drowning in the others' failure.

Tim was the first to go under. He was a short man, his loose skin a reminder of a life in which food was plentiful. He spoke little, preferring to make his noise in song. He had a beautiful voice—some said he was once a professional singer—and when he sang troubles melted.

William had found him sprawled behind a dumpster, his fading cough speckling blood across his chest. Tristan helped to carry him back to the basement, where they laid him on the couch. William knelt beside the dying man the whole afternoon, holding his hand and filling his ear with comforting lies.

Tim died as night fell, with the group watching over him. He was neither young nor old, in his forties Tristan guessed—too young to die. It had come suddenly, there had been no sign of illness, yet no one expressed surprise. Tristan looked down on the body and felt his own death waiting, fixed at that point where his future ended, drawing him ever nearer. He felt himself expanding with the need to scream but there was no one, nothing to scream at.

Tristan felt a hand on his shoulder. He turned to see Fat Annie leaning close. She motioned for him to follow her out of earshot of the group.

'Are you all right?'

'I'm better than him,' Tristan replied, tasting the bitterness on his tongue.

'You need to be calm now, Tristan,' Annie told him. 'We have a job for you. The time has come for you to help us.'

'How?' he asked.

'I need you to help me with the burying.'

'I can help with the digging,' Tristan offered.

'No. I mean with the prayers. Death requires a holy man.'

'No.' Tristan shook his head. 'It wouldn't be right.'

'You lead us in prayers all the time.'

'That's in fun, when there's been drinking.'

'There'll be drinking tonight,' she said. 'I can promise that.'

'I mean it's just play-acting. What I do is just play-acting.'

'We're all acting,' she replied. 'Look at me. Do you think this is who I am?'

That was exactly what he thought: that all her life she had sat upon her faded throne, massive and poor.

'But I don't believe any more, Annie.'

Tristan didn't know if this was true or not. He didn't know anything.

'Then you must pretend,' Annie told him, immovable as ever. 'What sort of barbarian doesn't pretend, in a time of death?'

'Why does there have to be death?' Tristan replied, knowing at once how foolish he sounded.

'I don't know, Tristan. What did Augustine say?'

'It's not what I mean.'

'What are you saying?' Fat Annie's eyes darted away. He'd never seen them do that before.

'Why do we just let them die?'

'We?'

'You then.' Anger came on him without warning and Tristan let it flow. 'Why not organise ourselves properly? We could find more fuel if we had a system. I walked past a building site yesterday. With twenty men we could empty it in a night and be warm for a month. It's…this place, it's haphazard. You just leave people to wander where they will. There is food to be had behind the restaurants, but they change their routines to foil us. If we had people watching all the time, then we'd—'

'Shhh, boy. Shhh.' His raised voice had brought attention to them. Annie pulled Tristan close and placed a hand across his mouth. She rocked him against her shoulder as if he was a child. The others, satisfied it was grief they had heard, turned back to the body.

'It's not how we do it here, Tristan,' she whispered.

'Why not?' he demanded.

'Because they are not fighters.'

'They fight all the time.'

'With each other, not with fate. That fight has gone out of them.'

Tristan knew there was no point. She understood where this argument would lead as well as he did. All the way back to Augustine and the free will they could no longer believe in. Annie rubbed his back and her voice softened.

'I could try what you say, Tristan, but how long do you think it would last? One week maybe, or two, before it fell apart. Do you think that's what they need right now, more hope followed by failure?'

'So you offer hopelessness instead?'

'I don't offer anything, Tristan. They come to me.'

'You can't just accept this,' Tristan said.

'We all die, Tristan. The believer and the nonbeliever alike.'

'No. You're wrong. You make us sound like animals. We're not. We're not just animals!' It wasn't her argument, he knew that, but there was no one else he could throw it at.

'No, Tristan, we're not just animals. Look at your friend. Look at William.'

Tristan turned back to the group. Where others stood awkwardly, half turned from the corpse, hoping to hide in a sputtering conversation, William had eyes only for his fallen friend. It was over an hour since Tim's heart had stopped, yet William remained perched at the edge of the couch, his long frame unfolded over his friend, his warm cheek resting on the cold face of death. Tristan watched a bony hand move slowly across Tim's face, stroking an eyebrow, the nose, the lips.

'Come on,' Annie whispered. 'Get your prayers ready. A brother needs burying.'

That night Tristan performed the first of the season's burial ceremonies. Uttering prayers he barely believed over men he hardly knew was to become his special role. They dug holes when they could, but the winter ground was hard and for every man on the shovel another was needed to stand guard, watching for the authorities, who insisted on taking corpses away for burning. When the grave was ready word would spread and the mourners would arrive: sometimes as many as thirty, other times a smaller, sadder number.

No two funerals were the same. Drink, old enmities, even the weather could nudge the story from its path. Still a ritual of sorts emerged. Someone, usually but not always a friend, would attempt to take on the voice of the deceased and tell his favourite story. There was drinking, naturally, and often a fight. More than once an enthusiastic mourner climbed down into the hole and had to be dragged back amongst the living. Eventually the energy would seep from the gathering just as it had seeped from the departed, and Tristan would recite the prayers. Then those who knew the deceased best would drop a few of his favourite things onto the body: a flask perhaps, a syringe, a battered copy of a book he had carried, once even the body of a small dog— the donor swore it had not been sacrificed for the ceremony but nobody believed him. Some insisted on a tradition they claimed had its roots in antiquity and pissed on the body before filling the hole back in.

No ceremony took place without Fat Annie's contribution, usually a short eulogy in which she displayed a remarkable ability to remember the departed as they would have wished to be remembered. Annie was the tugging mass at the centre of their makeshift world and they couldn't imagine it turning without her.

But it did.

Tristan woke shivering. It had become his habit to lie beside Annie, for warmth, he told himself, but this morning the great lump had turned cold. At first he registered only that there was something wrong: noises and shadows his sleepy mind couldn't piece together. Dazzling white shafts diffracted through the ventilation slots; shouting jostled in the air. Tristan rose slow and muddle-headed, aware that the noise was getting closer. By the time he had gained his senses a terrible wailing was pulsing through the emptiness.

He turned back to Annie and saw death painted on her face. Her lips had turned thin and dry, and her wide eyes were empty of understanding. Instinctively Tristan wrapped his arms around her. Just when he had come to believe he had nothing left to lose, here he was, falling again.

It took them a full day to agree on a course of action. They could all claim to be Annie's friend, and that left everything open to disagreement. William perhaps was the closest to her but he was reluctant to assert his privileges. She had shown Tristan a special regard, it was true, but he was too recent an arrival. Some turned to Little Cam, the remaining purrer, but all he had to offer was his fervent wish to take her place in the hole.

They all understood that when they buried Annie they would bury their fragile peace, and the funeral negotiation became a cautious, trustless affair.

They talked themselves to drink and eventually sleep, with Fat Annie's body cold on the ground. The next morning one of the men made good a drunken promise and returned with a work gang to which he had once belonged. They used a jackhammer to break up the concrete where she lay. The idea was to make a mausoleum of their shabby home. The workers left them to dig the hole. It took a team of ten the rest of the morning. Then they levered her into her grave.

There was much anguish and accusation when Fat Annie landed heavily, face-down, offering the world her preposterous rump in farewell. The brawl between those who wished to turn her and those who wished to leave her as she lay was fierce and they were lucky not to have needed a second grave. The turners won the battle, but lost the war; Fat Annie's weight and the snugness of the fit foiled their attempts to move her.

Mourners came from all around, and by the middle of the afternoon hundreds filled the basement. The vagrant army shuffled through the space like penguins; without prompting they had happened upon a system of spiralling that ensured each a turn at the centre to gaze on the body. Tristan moved through the warmth and stench with William at his side. Even if he had wanted to escape he couldn't have. The crowd moved as one, unwinding its grief as the day ran down.

Five times Tristan found himself at the centre and each time the hole had changed a little: tokens dropped, regathered, stolen, rearranged. On the third pass he noted that the body had been turned. Later, they would all swear no one saw her moved, that a miracle had occurred.

There was no ceremony because they had not been able to agree on the details. Somewhere in the shrunken hours the crowd began to thin. People left without farewell just as they had arrived without welcome. The only ones still circling were those with nowhere else to go. Little Cam walked a circuit beside Tristan and when they reached the open grave he said, 'Do you think there should be a prayer now?'

Tristan looked at the boy then down to Annie. He knew no words to bring her fleshy face back from the dirt.

'Would you like one?'

'Yes, please.'

There were fewer than twenty people left in the basement and the sound of the prayer drew them together. Tristan spoke the words slowly, automatically, feeling only their echoing emptiness:

> Lord, you teach us that in death you embrace us.
> In trial you carry us, in uncertainty you guide us
> and in sorrow you comfort us. We ask you now
> to embrace our friend Annie, as she embraced
> life. We ask you to welcome her into your home
> and to give us the strength to live in a world of
> loss, a world held together by your great love.
> We cannot know your ways, Lord, but we ask for
> the courage to accept your plan for us. For the
> woman we knew, we thank you, and for the hope
> you offer us, we thank you. Amen.

A long silence was broken by the clang of a shovel on concrete and they began filling the hole. William approached Tristan.

'You need to take over now,' William said. 'It's what she would have wanted.'

'No,' Tristan replied. 'There is nothing left here. It is finished.'

'What will you do?' William asked.

'I don't know.' As he spoke the words Tristan felt his sadness grow heavy within him. 'I have never known.'

§

Tristan's head throbbed and his vision, still without colour, held its focus only in moments before returning him to a world of floating debris. Talking had become a terrible drain but there was no denying the story's momentum. He took her hand. Soon she would push him away.

'I don't know if you will understand what happened next.'

'Try me.'

'Sometimes you think you understand a thing—you can turn it into words and the words seem to make sense—but then true understanding arrives, and you realise that all you'd ever seen before was the shadow of the idea. Death was not new to me, and I understood that even Annie would one day return to dirt. But to see her there, so completely reduced, when only a day before it had been impossible to imagine our world without her…

'Something left me then. Not hope, but the thing hope rests upon. Belief. William walked away without saying goodbye, as if he had already sensed I was gone. I watched the shovels of dirt land heavily on her body and I felt nothing. I was nothing. I had nothing. I drifted into the path of the oncoming day.

'For three days I staggered through the streets. I stopped eating. I was fading into certainty. You know those streets, you know how full of life they are, but I couldn't see it. All I could see was a thousand balls, each rolling through the maze: people reduced to movement, movement reduced to pattern. The rector had tried to explain it to me, but even at my lowest moment I hadn't properly understood. Not until those slow dying days, when the knowledge became a part of me. I would have died. There is no doubting it. I walked without eating or drinking, but the physical fatigue was such a small part of my pain that I barely noticed it.

'And then I saw you.'

'I don't remember,' she said. There had been a change in her silence. As if she sensed how close she was to knowledge.

'There was nothing about me you would have noticed. I was just another beggar fallen on the far side of a street you had no business in. I could see, though, from the way you walked, that you had fallen too.'

'When was it?'

'Three days ago.'

There was pause as she struggled to remember. 'It was raining,' she said.

'This was before the rain. It was afternoon.'

'I was going to work.'

'I know. I followed you. I didn't mean to. But there was no mistaking you, even at that distance. My heart lurched in the familiar way, a distant, nostalgic sensation I was too thick-headed to make sense of. I left my few possessions on the street wrapped in a blanket, and I followed you.'

'You should have called out.'

'It's becoming our theme,' he said, but neither of them smiled.

'I'm sorry,' Tristan continued. 'I don't know if I can explain this. I walked helplessly along the path you laid. Slowly, as if fighting my way through mud. My mind was sticky with the memory of another night in another world, when I should have…But I'd stopped believing in should.

'A strange thing happened as I walked behind you. For the first time in days my fragmented self moved with a single purpose. No, not a purpose, a yearning. A memory. You found your place beneath the canopy just before the rain came. I was huddled in an alley opposite. I whimpered when you removed your coat. A rat beneath a pile of boxes scurried at the sound, instinct taking it deeper into the maze.

'Do you remember the car that stopped? It was long and black with silver spokes in its wheels. I didn't see him, but I shouted as you drove away. "Don't hurt her, you bastard," I called out like a madman.

'As the car moved off, I felt as if the last piece of the puzzle was sliding into place. You turned a corner and disappeared from view, and my life turned rigid again. I did not move, I could not move, but I thought of him, the stranger in the car with money in his pocket and flesh on his mind. I had never properly met you, we had never spoken, and yet I knew that if he harmed you I would hunt him down. Just imagining it filled me with a rage that could never fade to forgiveness.

'And that, that single realisation, completes the puzzle. Do you see ? Do you understand?'

Tristan waited but Grace gave no sign of having heard the question. He did not blame her. It had taken him too long to see it as well.

'Remember what the rector told me? *If none of us is responsible, then none of us is past forgiveness.* He had planted it there, don't you see, the solution to my conundrum. Only the free act can be unforgivable. I stood alone on a wet street and watched you drive away, and I finally understood. To commit the unforgivable act is to be free. And it wasn't too late. It's never too late.'

His words tumbled together, a muddy mash of reason and desperation. *You are crazy*, she would be thinking. *You have lost your mind.* But that was the opposite of the truth. It was the exact opposite.

'I did not have a car, or the money to pay for one. But I had an obsession and I would not be denied. The suit I'm wearing belongs to a businessman who swims each morning at the public pool. The car is hired under his name. That part wasn't difficult. The difficult part comes now. The difficult part is in the explaining.'

She had gone still beside him but he knew she was listening. For a moment he felt powerful again. A fierceness came over him, a kind of determination he had experienced only once before. It was happening.

'You are it, Grace. You are my destiny. From the moment I first saw you I knew this simple truth. When the car pulled away, the fear of you being harmed found its way to my core. I could never conceive of it, Grace. I could never even think of hurting you.'

'Do not say it.'

'To hurt you would be unforgivable. I could no more doubt this than I could doubt the existence of my own hand. And that is how I could prove him wrong.'

'You are mad. This is the talk of a madman!'

'I did not choose you, Grace. Fate chose you. And I chose to deny my fate.

'I drove the block twice tonight, the first time just to look at you, the second to harden my resolve. You could not have guessed at the mighty urges that clawed and writhed within me. I smiled at you. You smiled back and my heart soared. I wanted to save you. I wanted to save us both.

'I chose the road carefully. I drove it earlier today: I needed to be sure. The corners came fast, each folding into the next, pushing back a little harder. It is addictive, the thrill of speed, approaching that point where skill and danger are delicately balanced. I heard your breathing quicken with my heart. You wanted to speak out, to ask me to slow down. But you did not. As if it was written. As if you knew.

'I felt my history rising up against me, urging me to caution. I beat it back. I have never faced a more daunting opponent but my resolve was strong. I denied my love for you. I say "I", but now we see the word is no longer adequate. I speak of something more, of will alone. It pulled at the wheel, fought against the road. The car lost traction. I accelerated. Did you feel it? There was no ice.

'I meant to commit the unforgivable act, Grace. I meant to kill us both.'

'But you didn't kill me,' she said. 'I am still here.'

Tristan took her throat in his hands and felt it soften beneath his thumbs. He pressed down, feeling the corrugations of her windpipe, experimenting with its elasticity. She stared grey-faced back at him, treating him at last to the hatred he had earned.

'So this is how you do it, is it?' she hissed. He pushed harder, and she made no move to fight him. 'You would rather choke an argument than counter it.'

'You have no argument,' he said.

'I do. You're just not willing to hear it.'

He loosened the pressure; her rasping was too terrible to bear.

'We all know we will die, Tristan,' she said. 'Dying doesn't frighten me. But I always thought it would be for something more noble than one man's vanity.'

He closed his one good eye against her accusation.

'You won't do it,' Grace taunted, sensing the fraying of him.

'Why won't I?'

He looked at her again. Her lip curled back, revealing the gap in her teeth. She snarled.

'Let me go, Tristan. Let me go. It's not too late.'

'Too late for what?'

'Learning from our mistakes.'

'I am not mistaken,' he insisted.

'So why are you shaking?'

'Talk and I will listen,' he said, regretting at once the bargain. But how could he demand she stop talking when all he craved was the sound of her voice? 'But be quick. My fingers know what they must do.'

'I cannot speak like this.'

'Then do not speak.' He pushed harder, tasting blood in his mouth, his throat, his imagination. She spat at him. He felt its warmth slide thickly on his cheek.

'I hate you for this.'

'You should,' he replied. 'You must.'

She leaned into him and he felt her weight straining against his fingers. Her face was too close for him to make out any more than her burning eyes.

'Do you think any but the St Augustine's student thinks twice about the nature of his will?' she challenged. 'Do you think there are any others who have the luxury of giving a shit? I knew a girl on the street called Francis. She died of a cough because she couldn't afford medicine. Each evening she faced the same choice: whether or not to risk the cold of the streets in search of the money that might keep at bay the symptoms of that coldness. I sat with her as she died and she described snippets of her childhood. Not once was her fading mind troubled by Augustine's stupid paradoxes. But now you lie here with your fingers to my throat, seeking to make some college boy's point that means nothing to either of us. And all because you were too frightened to talk to me. If I die now it is only because you are a coward.'

He bit his tongue, whether hard enough to make it bleed he could not tell. All was blood now. All was pain.

'He knew!' Tristan roared, so loud that it felt as if his own throat might be shredded by it, but she did not recoil. He shook her head and heard the dull thud of bone on metal.

She stared back, refusing to be moved by his tantrum. 'Before I decided, he knew how I would decide! How can that not matter? How can that not be the end of us?'

'You said it yourself!' she screamed in return, as if hoping her voice might pierce his certainty. 'You used the word. Decided. You still decided. You made a choice. A choice between two paths.'

'But one of them wasn't open to me.'

'I don't know what that means,' she said. 'And neither do you.'

'It means it was never going to happen.'

She rolled her eyes and her disdain triggered a moment of uncertainty in him.

'And what would it be like,' she challenged, 'this world where alternative paths remained open even after the event had happened? It is incoherent. And now you want to kill me because you hope it will let you believe in a world neither of us can even imagine?'

His felt her words vibrating through his hands. The argument surprised him. Not its vigour—who wouldn't defend their right to breathe—but its subtlety. It unsettled him that a lifetime's learning could be met so easily by an untrained mind.

'There is a difference.' His voice was shaking and he felt his hands tighten, urging its silence. Tears stung his eyes. He did not want this, he did not want it done. 'The rector knew my mind before I knew it myself. I felt I was choosing the path, but the path had already chosen me. That is my point.'

'Then your point is hollow,' Grace said. 'Where is the loss

in behaving in a way that is predictable? The finest people I have ever met have been the most predictable. It speaks of their character, that in the face of life's challenges their values still shine through. You shrink from predictability when you should aspire to it.'

'There is no point in aspiring to anything,' Tristan replied, 'if success or failure is determined in advance.'

'And what is the alternative to this determinism?' she screamed. 'You said it, Tristan. The alternative is disorder. You can be wilful or you can be free. You told me that. And now you choose chaos over purpose, death over love.'

From the first time he had seen her, this had been her way. She could reshape the world before his eyes, making every familiar thing strange.

'So how are we any different from the balls in the cradle?' Tristan asked. 'Tell me that.'

His hands shook so violently he wasn't sure he could control them. He saw the grotesque swelling of his knuckles, and couldn't believe they were part of him. But he did not tighten his grip. He waited for her to answer. He wanted her to answer.

'We are different,' Grace said, 'because of the stories we tell ourselves, and the stories we tell each other. They contribute as much to our trajectories as the physics of our collisions. You and I are stuck here because of the stories your teachers told you. We are here because of the God you cannot stop believing in.'

'God is no part of my argument.'

'He is your whole argument,' she returned, 'and I am your

sacrifice. Don't you see? All the philosophy they taught you, it's just a game. An exercise in being clever, in twisting your thoughts into ever more elaborate patterns. But those games belong behind the walls of the monasteries and universities. To bring them out into the world is a kind of insanity.'

'That is a shallow argument.'

'You are right: I argue in favour of shallowness. I make choices, Tristan; so do you. I know this as clearly as I know the feel of rain on my face or the bright glare of sunshine. You have made the will disappear in the way a conjurer makes a rabbit vanish, and it is insanity to believe your own trickery. There is no magic in the world. There is no God. There is you and there is me and this car turned on its roof and above us, I would wager, some slab of rock obscuring us from view, because it is light now and if anyone on the road was to spot us it would have already happened. So kill me if you must, but don't think it makes you any more free. It can never be right, Tristan, that I should die for your vanity.'

He squeezed again, throttling her words, sending her into a spasm of choking. Her eyes bulged, lost and terrified. Again he relented and she coughed blood down at the ceiling. He could not do it. He could not kill the thing he loved. Defeat settled on him. He could not look at her.

'He was right,' Tristan muttered. 'I am not free.'

He heard her slump against the side of the car. He could feel her shaking and he thought he heard her crying. He wanted to hold her. He wanted his past back. He wanted her.

Tristan listened to the music of the world, the rise and fall of the wind, the insistent percussion of his heart, and somewhere in the distant world the small uncertain melody of a bird that held no opinion on their predicament. He listened to her breathing, slow again, and wondered at the strangeness of love that even now brought such joy at the sound of her recovering.

'You are free, Tristan,' she whispered. 'I can show you.'

'Don't,' he told her. 'Let the argument lie now. You have won.'

'Not yet,' she replied. 'We are still trapped.'

'I don't understand.'

'You say the choices we face are not real, but how about this one? If we stay here, there is a chance no one will see us. Perhaps one day they will come searching for their car, but we will be dead by then. Or I may be wrong. It may be just that no driver has looked down this way, or the sun is not yet high enough in the sky to mark our colour out amongst the rocks. Perhaps salvation is nearer than we dare hope.

'But we have tumbled this car before and we can do it again. If the drop to the bottom is small it won't hurt us more and it might move us to a place where we can be seen. If the fall is great then we will die trying to save ourselves. And that is a choice, isn't it? Imperfect, as all choices are, but how can you say we are not free when right now our future depends on it?'

He said nothing. He had no answer.

'So what do we do? Do we wait and hope, or do we try to rock the car from its resting place? This is not fate, Tristan. Nothing is determined and there is no rector here to tell us which way you will jump. There is just you and me, and life and death. You can reduce it to physics if you want to, but I will still ask you what you want to do, and you must still tell me. This is life, Tristan, yours and mine, the whole game resting on a simple choice, imperfect and constrained, as all choices are. Whether we live or die depends on this decision and there is nobody else here to make it for us.'

She paused, waiting for Tristan's response. He had nothing.

'You cannot argue we are not free, Tristan. Freedom is all we have. What do you want to do? Tell me and I will do it.'

Tristan laughed, a sudden release that took him by surprise, and she laughed too. Their monstrous sounds filled the cabin, a cackling bloody echo—two souls moved to a point past caring. Tristan felt the pain of his shaking body, but he couldn't stop it. Delirium took hold and he offered no resistance.

He felt light again. He reached out his hand and she met his fingertips with her own.

'What will it be?' she whispered.

Tristan considered the choice. He felt a tightening at his temples, the great vice of self-pity.

'I am frightened,' he said, hoping that naming the thing might diminish it, but his fear leaped at the word, inflating it to impossible proportions. 'I don't want to die.'

He waited.

'This is where you tell me we're not going to die,' he said.

'Do we wait here or do we move the car?' she pressed.

'It is not for me to decide.'

'One of us must.'

Tristan's mind froze, his thoughts caught on a Mobius strip of intention and denial. He turned away from the decision, hoping that it might resolve itself without him. Nothing. He looked at Grace, seeing for the first time how young she was. Hers was the face of a child waking from a nightmare, seeking out its parent. The decision was his.

The future split in two before him, each path lined with hope and shaded by death. He closed his eyes and waited. Slowly, surely, the decision settled over him. He breathed it in, until he and the decision were one.

'We do it,' he whispered to her. 'We move the car.'

'Are you waiting for me?' Grace asked.

'Yes.'

'I'm waiting for you.'

'It could take a while then.'

'Yes.'

'Is there something we should say, do you think?' Tristan asked.

'A prayer?' she replied.

'I don't know. Isn't there one last thing you want to tell the world?'

'It's not a last thing. They'll see us. They'll come.'

'So we are to die in denial?'

'It's how we live.'

She took his hand. Her fingers crushed his knuckles.

They began to rock together, so slowly that at first he was not sure it had begun. His body moved with hers. The car shifted its weight. He heard metal stressing beneath him, and felt the softness of her body melting into his. He pushed back.

'More!'

She crushed into him. He resisted, bracing with his legs. He let go, screaming now as she was, seeking out every last scrap of rage.

Suddenly she was on top of him, then he on her.

They were floating, tumbling together in a machine not made for tumbling, weightless and free. He considered the physics: gravity recast as acceleration. An odd thought to have, but what thought isn't odd when death breathes close and sticky? The world slowed. He looked at her. They were free.

Also by Bernard Beckett from Quercus:

GENESIS

Turn the page to read an extract.

A nax moved down the long corridor. The only sound was the gentle hiss of the air filter overhead. The lights were down low, as demanded by the new regulations. She remembered brighter days, but never spoke of them. It was one of the Great Mistakes, thinking of brightness as a quality of the past.

Anax reached the end of the corridor and turned left. She checked the time. They would be watching her approach, or so it was rumoured. The door slid open, quiet and smooth, like everything in The Academy zone.

'Anaximander?'

Anax nodded.

The panel was made up of three Examiners, just as the regulations had promised. It was a great relief. Details of the examination were kept secret, and among the candidates rumours swirled. 'Imagination is the bastard child of time and ignorance,' her tutor Pericles liked to say, always adding 'not that I have anything against bastards.'

Anax loved her tutor. She would not let him down. The door closed behind her.

The Examiners sat behind a high desk, the top a dark slab of polished timber.

'Make yourself comfortable.' The Examiner in the middle spoke. He was the largest of the three, as tall and broad as any Anax had ever seen. By comparison the other two looked old and weak, but she felt their eyes upon her, keen and sharp. Today she would assume nothing. The space before them was clear. Anax knew the interview was being recorded.

EXAMINER: Four hours have been allotted for your examination. You may seek clarification, should you have trouble understanding any of our questions, but the need to do this will be taken into consideration when the final judgment is made. Do you understand this?

ANAXIMANDER: Yes.

EXAMINER: Is there anything you would like to ask, before we begin?

ANAXIMANDER: I would like to ask you what the answers are.

EXAMINER: I'm sorry. I don't quite understand...

ANAXIMANDER: I was joking.

EXAMINER: Oh. I see.

A bad idea. Not so much as a flicker of acknowledgment from any of them. Anax wondered whether she should apologise, but the gap closed quickly over.

EXAMINER: Anaximander, your time begins now. Four hours on your chosen subject. The life and times of Adam Forde, 2058–2077. Adam Forde was born seven years into the age of Plato's Republic. Can you please explain to us the political circumstances that led to The Republic's formation?

Was this a trick? Anax's topic clearly stated her area of expertise covered the years of Adam's life only. The proposal had been accepted by the committee without amendment. She knew a little of the political background of course, everybody did, but it was not her area of expertise. All she could offer was a classroom recitation, familiar to every student. This was no way to start. Should she challenge it? Were they expecting her to challenge it? She looked to their faces for clues, but they sat impassive as stone, offering her nothing.

EXAMINER: Anaximander, did you understand the question?

ANAXIMANDER: Of course I did. I'm sorry. I'm just... it doesn't matter...

Anax tried to clear her mind of worries. Four hours. Plenty of time to show how much she knew.

ANAXIMANDER: The story begins at the end of the third decade of the new millennium. As with any age, there was no shortage of doomsayers. Early attempts at genetic engineering had frightened large sectors of the community. The international economy was still oil-based, and the growing consensus was that a catastrophic shortage loomed.

What was then known as the Middle East remained a politically troubled region, and the United States—I will use the designations of the time for consistency—was seen by many to have embroiled itself in a war it could not win, with a culture it did not understand. While it promoted its interests as those of democracy, the definition was narrow and idiosyncratic, and made for a poor export.

Fundamentalism was on the rise on both sides of this divide, and the first clear incidents of Western Terrorism in Saudi Arabia in 2032 were seen by many as the spark for a fire that would never be doused. Europe was accused of having lost its moral compass and the independence riots of 2047 were seen as further evidence of secular decay. China's rise to international prominence, and what it called 'active diplomacy', led many to fear that another global conflict was on the horizon. Economic expansion threatened the global environment. Biodiversity shrank at unprecedented rates, and the last opponents of the Accelerated Climate Change Model were converted to the cause by the dust storms of 2041. In short, the world faced many challenges, and by the end of the fifth decade of the current century, public discourse was dominated by a mood of threat and pessimism.

It is, of course, easy to be wise with the benefit of hindsight, but from our vantage point it is now clear that the only thing the population had to fear was fear itself. The true danger humanity faced during this period was the shrinking of its own spirit.

EXAMINER: Define spirit.

The Examiner's voice was carefully modulated, the sort of effect that could be achieved with the cheapest of filters. Only it wasn't technology Anax heard; it was control, pure and simple.

Every pause, every flickering of uncertainty: the Examiners observed them all. This, surely, was how they decided. Anax felt suddenly slow and unimpressive. She could still hear Pericles' last words. 'They want to see how you will respond to the challenge. Don't hesitate. Talk your way towards understanding. Trust the words.' And back then it had sounded so simple. Now her face tautened and she had to think her way to the words, searching for them in the way one searches for a friend in a crowd, panic never more than a moment away.

ANAXIMANDER: By spirit I mean to say something about the prevailing mood of the time. Human spirit is the ability to face the uncertainty of the future with curiosity and optimism. It is the belief that problems can be solved, differences resolved. It is a type of confidence. And it is fragile. It can be blackened by fear, and superstition. By the year 2050, when the conflict began, the world had fallen upon fearful, superstitious times.

EXAMINER: Tell us more about these superstitions.

ANAXIMANDER: Superstition is the need to view the world in terms of simple cause and effect. As I have already said, religious fundamentalism was on the rise, but that is not the type of superstition I'm referring to. The superstition that held sway at the time was a belief in simple causes.

Even the plainest of events is tied down by a thick tangle of permutation and possibility, but the human mind struggles with such complexity. In times of trouble, when the belief in simple gods breaks down, a cult of conspiracy arises. So it was back then. Unable to attribute misfortune to chance, unable to accept their ultimate insignificance within the greater scheme, the people looked for monsters in their midst.

The more the media peddled fear, the more the people lost the ability to believe in one another. For every new ill that befell them, the media created an explanation, and the explanation always had a face and a name. The people came to fear even their closest neighbours. At the level of the individual, the community and the nation, people sought signs of others' ill intentions; and everywhere they looked, they found them, for this is what looking does.

This was the true challenge the people of this time faced. The challenge of trusting each other. And they fell short of this challenge. This is what I mean, when I say they faced a shrinking of the spirit.

EXAMINER: Thank you for your clarification. Now please return to your story of the times. How did The Republic come to be established?

Just as Pericles had predicted, Anax was buoyed by the sound of her own voice. This is what made her such a good candidate. Her thoughts followed her words, or so he explained it. 'Everybody is different, and this is your skill.' So although the story she was telling was a stale one, left too long, examined too often, Anax found herself wrapping it in new words, growing in confidence with every layer.